On the
Blue Comet

On the Blue Comet

ROSEMARY WELLS

ILLUSTRATED BY

BAGRAM IBATOULLINE

WALKER
BOOKS

For Victoria Wells Arms
R. W.

First published in Great Britain 2010 by Walker Books Ltd
87 Vauxhall Walk, London, SE11 5HJ

2 4 6 8 10 9 7 5 3 1

Text © 2010 Rosemary Wells
Illustrations © 2010 Bagram Ibatoulline

The right of Rosemary Wells and Bagram Ibatoulline
to be identified as author and illustrator of this work
respectively has been asserted by them in accordance with
the Copyright, Designs and Patents Act 1988

This book has been typeset in Bembo.
The illustrations were done in acrylic gouache.

Printed and bound in Crawfordsville, IN, USA.

British Library Cataloguing in Publication Data:
a catalogue record for this book is
available from the British Library

ISBN 978-1-4063-3014-4

www.walker.co.uk

If

If you can keep your head when all about you
Are losing theirs and blaming it on you,
If you can trust yourself when all men doubt you,
But make allowance for their doubting too;
If you can wait and not be tired by waiting,
Or, being lied about, don't deal in lies,
Or, being hated, don't give way to hating,
And yet don't look too good, nor talk too wise;

If you can dream — and not make dreams your master;
If you can think — and not make thoughts your aim,
If you can meet with Triumph and Disaster
And treat those two impostors just the same;
If you can bear to hear the truth you've spoken
Twisted by knaves to make a trap for fools,
Or watch the things you gave your life to broken,
And stoop and build 'em up with worn-out tools;

If you can make one heap of all your winnings
And risk it on one turn of pitch-and-toss,
And lose, and start again at your beginnings
And never breath a word about your loss;
If you can force your heart and nerve and sinew
To serve your turn long after they are gone,
And so hold on when there is nothing in you
Except the Will which says to them: "Hold on";

If you can talk with crowds and keep your virtue,
Or walk with kings — nor lose the common touch;
If neither foes nor loving friends can hurt you;
If all men count with you, but none too much;
If you can fill the unforgiving minute
With sixty seconds' worth of distance run,
Yours is the earth and everything that's in it,
And — which is more — you'll be a Man, my son!

Rudyard Kipling

CHAPTER 1

We lived at the end of Lucifer Street, on the Mississippi River side of Cairo, Illinois. Black spruces lined our sandy road. My heart quickened as I watched my dad lope home over the fallen needles. Bouncing along on his shoulder was a red cardboard box labeled **LIONEL COMPANY, ROCHESTER, NEW YORK.** In that box was my birthday present, the Blue Comet. The Blue Comet was the queen of all trains.

I waited for him under the porch light. The forty-watt yellow bulb made a Grand Central Station for flapping moths and zizzing june bugs above my head. In the kitchen, our dinner was warm and fragrant on the stove.

The house at the end of Lucifer Street had been my mama's great joy. She fixed it up so pretty when I was just a baby, all yellow curtains and shiny white trim. We have a lone portrait, its edges curled, of me, Dad, and Mama. I was just a skinny, freckled little boy of three in that Brownie camera snapshot, with a cowlick pointing straight up out of the top of my head.

Mama was the bookkeeper in the Lucifer Fireworks plant until one day a bolt of walking lightning shot right through the shipping-room window, stopping the clock and sizzling into a box of Roman candles near her chair. Everyone would say afterward she had not known or felt a thing in that half-second explosion. All I remember seeing was a fire truck out the window of our kitchen and my aunt Carmen, who had appeared from nowhere, covering my eyes with her hands.

What was left of the Lucifer factory was declared unsafe and closed down soon after. You might think my dad would want to move away from Lucifer Street and the terrible reminders of the accident.

But in the end he could not bear to leave the yellow curtains and white trim that Mama had painted herself. He certainly did not wish to move into the Chateaux Apartment Village as Aunt Carmen, his in-town sister, suggested. Aunt Carmen was always telling Dad what he ought to do.

"Get your life back on the tracks and find a good woman, Oscar," Aunt Carmen whispered loudly to Dad every time she had the littlest chance. "The boy needs a mother, and you need a wife to keep your hair short and make you some casserole dinners."

"That goes double, Carmen," my dad always replied. Aunt Carmen lived alone in a little house full of bisque figurines. Squirrel silhouettes were cut into the house's shutters. It was explained to me that Aunt Carmen had never married because the Great War had taken the lives of so many young men that there were not enough to go around.

"A good man is a darn sight harder to find than a good woman," Aunt Carmen always answered my dad with a sniff.

Oftentimes a picture floated through my mind of the wife that Aunt Carmen had in mind for us. She looked like the lady on the Coca-Cola calendar, black hair parted on the side, dress with the stripes going across diamond-wise, big red lips showing off her white teeth.

"I will never be so lucky again as to find anyone like your mother," Dad said. "A new wife would make trouble and get in the way." What he meant was she would have gotten in the way of the trains in our basement.

Instead Dad and I lived a peaceful life, with me, Oscar Jr., in charge of cooking just as soon as I could reach the stove. In second grade, I was big enough, standing on a sturdy chair, to flip our Sunday pancakes and fry our breakfast sausage. Our weekly menu was casserole-free.

This is what it looked like:

> *Monday: Lamb chops and fried potatoes*
> *Tuesday: Fried chicken, canned green beans,*
>   *fried potatoes*
> *Wednesday: Hamburger, fried potatoes, and tomatoes*
> *Thursday: Hot dogs and beans*
> *Friday: Beefsteak and carrots*
> *Saturday: Pork chops and cabbage*
> *Sunday: Ham and gravy with pineapple rings*

The menu never changed from week to week because it satisfied. There was just enough variety to keep us from getting bored but nothing like liver or spinach to scare us away.

I bought all our groceries at Rubin's Market after school, charging them to our account. Then I walked the groceries home, set them on the counter, and began to prepare our evening meal.

We did just fine on our own, Dad and me. Dad had a steady job with the John Deere Company, selling tractors to the farmers. He even had a telephone installed right in the front hall, much to the dismay of Aunt Carmen. For my part, I kept my shoes shined, and my homework was always finished. Dad and I agreed: we had no need whatever of a new wife. So that wife never did happen. It was just as well. A wife would have been putting on her lipstick all the time and giving me cod-liver oil.

In the beginning, Dad had set up our first layout to pull himself out of the widower doldrums. It was a simple one-looper. He made the station out of basswood, painted pumpkin yellow just like the real railway station in downtown Cairo. He cut eight little signs and painted them white with CAIRO in

blue, just as it was on the real signs. I hung them off the eaves of the station's shingled roof with chrome-beaded key chains. We laid eastward tracks and westward tracks. The track beds were made of carefully dribbled bird gravel on a layer of carpenter's glue.

Then Dad ordered signals and an electrically operated gate out of the Lionel catalog to go with our first train, a standard work train. Dad took a sable brush that had maybe six hairs to it. He painted SOO LINE HAPPY WARRIOR on the side of the engine in red paint, exactly like on the real Soo Line. Our Happy Warrior had a lumber car with logs as long as cigarillos, two cattle cars, a coaler, a caboose, and a refrigerator car that had small cubes of glass ice inside, each no bigger than one of my Parcheesi dice.

The Warrior was followed by a commuter train, which we called the South Shore Special. We ran it from Chicago to the dunes of Indiana and back. The passenger cars were rigged with real electric lights inside. We put together three stop stations on that commuter express. They came from the Ives Company, which made the most detailed stations.

Then Dad bought us the biggest steam engine in the catalog. It was a 260 series with marker lights on each side, one red, one green. There was a red light underneath the boiler that made the coals glow. The trim was copper and brass, the wheels had spoked drivers with nickel rims. It carried freight cars and three passenger Pullmans. We named it the Choctaw Rocket of the Rock Island Line. Our first tabletop layout was now too small. We began constructing the mountains of the west, lumping up their foothills out of stiff window screening. We layered plaster of paris on top of that, and then we painted it granite gray. This was sprinkled with sand, glue, and a green mystery powder provided by the Cairo druggist, Hop Shumway.

"You're not going to swallow this stuff, are you, Oscar?" Hop Shumway asked my dad, pushing a box of the green powder across the drugstore counter.

"On the contrary, Hop," Dad answered. "We're going to make the Transcontinental Railroad," and we did.

The benchwork for the mountains, canyons, and bridges that ran between was constructed of wooden crossbeams, like the criss-cross supports of a roller coaster. A tunnel ran through the mountains. The river that coursed under the trestle bridge was painted blue over silvery tinfoil. The ripples were transparent lines of model airplane glue. The tracks shot down the length and a whole side of our basement. Soon we had two tables and three tunnels.

"You are stark raving crazy, Oscar," Aunt Carmen said when she came to Thanksgiving dinner and asked what was in the basement that smelled of shellac. My cousin, Willa Sue, donkey's years younger than me, gazed at the layout in bewilderment.

"Don't touch anything. You might get electrocuted, Willa Sue," said Aunt Carmen.

"I can show you how the trains run," I said to Willa Sue encouragingly, even though I didn't like her much. Willa Sue had come to Aunt Carmen from a sister who was almost never mentioned. Once I overheard that Willa Sue's real mother might pull herself together one day and reappear, but this had never happened, and Willa Sue called Aunt Carmen *Mama* from day one. She was a cherub-mouthed girl and always had ahold of Aunt Carmen's skirt with one hand. The thumb of her other hand hovered, nearing her mouth, just as Aunt Carmen, quick as a mousing cat, pounced on the thumb and pushed it back down.

"Keep your hands at home, Willa Sue, dear," said Aunt Carmen.

"Girls don't like trains," whined Willa Sue. The thumb darted into the red bow mouth and stayed there a full thirty seconds while Aunt Carmen gave my dad a piece of her mind about his paycheck going down the drain on electric trains and throwing good money after bad on more and more electric trains.

"That's the Transcontinental Railroad you're talking about, Carmen," said my dad with a chuckle in his voice and a hand steady and warm on the back of my shirt collar. Then Dad lit a Muriel panatela so that Carmen and Willa Sue would go upstairs again.

I, myself, could not decide if the summer or the winter evenings were my favorites. I was grateful to have both.

From April through September, we got the Cubs and Cardinals games on the radio. We caught the play by play down in the basement, while the trains ran their routes in the cool shadows.

If you looked up through the two high-up-the-wall windows, you could watch the long summer evenings fade slowly. When we needed air, we opened the windows and the hot wind of the central plains rushed in.

"You can smell the alfalfa all the way from Kansas on that wind," Dad claimed, while he and I worked on switches, track repair, and new equipment installation.

In 1928, Dad sold a passel of tractors. And seldom did a week go by without a red box, or even two, arriving from the Lionel Company in Rochester, New York. Inside the train-set boxes was always a paper engineer's cap with blue and white stripes and a set of printed Lionel tickets for the route of the train inside. I never wore the hats because I thought they were for babies, but the tickets were printed in color and looked like the real thing. I collected them and kept at least a dozen wadded in an elastic band in my wallet.

On winter evenings, the sun set before I came home from school and before Dad came home from John Deere. We had our supper and talked about the work lying ahead that evening. Then we turned out all the lights in the house and went downstairs. On moonless nights, you might not have known from standing on Lucifer Street that our house was there at all. The wind soughed through the lonely spruces, much as I reckoned an Alaska wind might blow. Deep in our basement Dad and I stood together, wrapped on all sides by trains racing this way and that way, their smoke pellets pouring smoke, headlights shining down their tracks.

"Listen to that whistle," Dad told me many a time. "I hear that same whistle out in the farmland. The farmers hear it when they're taking in their hay. It goes right straight across the prairie all the way to Lincoln and beyond. Good people and bad hear it from inside the churches and prisons alike just as if it were the voice of the wolf."

"What is the voice of the wolf?" I asked.

Dad did not say.

Our Lionel trains corresponded exactly to the real trains in the big world. They were all modeled exactly on the genuine locomotive, freight cars, and Pullmans. Each was set up to stop at their stations, then to pull out and make their way up the Rocky Mountain ridges, over the Colorado River, and back through the tunnels to the South Side of Chicago. In the windless basement night, our transcontinental Golden State Limited crossed the plains from

Los Angeles to Chicago and back. The station lights winked as each train came through and the striped gate slammed down at the crossings.

By 1929 we owned ten complete trains. My favorite of all was the Blue Comet. Dad also judged it to be the finest of all the great Lionel trains. Her engine was sapphire blue, with a blue tender behind. Her passenger cars bore brass plates with the names of famous astronomers Westphal, Faye, and Barnard. The roofs came off if you wanted. Inside there were hinged doors, interior illumination, swiveling seats, and lavatories with cathedral ceilings.

Dad and I added an observation car to the back of the train. Dad took tweezers and turned two little blue seats right under the arc of the Plexiglas dome so that they were in perfect viewing position. "Someday, Oscar," my dad said, "we'll go to New York City and board the big Blue Comet, and these are the seats we'll reserve. The whole Atlantic shore will be spread before us, start to finish. We'll get out at Atlantic City. Then we can have our portraits painted on the boardwalk, and we can eat Turkish Taffy by the sea. Maybe for your next birthday!"

My next birthday came and went, and Dad and

I never did leave Cairo, but our imaginations took us up and down the continent and that was plenty enough for me. Sometimes I would place my head sideways, ear down, on the grass of the layout. "Are you sleepy, Oscar?" my dad always asked.

"No, just looking," I always answered. "Just looking."

What I was really doing was closing my bottom eye and staring with my top eye into the carriages of the passenger cars. The cars came complete with little cutout people, sitting in silhouette in each window. Here were two tiny tin women in hats, hands uplifted, chitchatting, both bent face to face. There a tin man read the newspaper. A tin boy ignored the porter, who stood above him with a tray, and gazed, two tiny pinholes for eyes, back out toward me. In this way, everything on the layout came to life, and I was no bigger than the people and the trains and buildings that stood in miniature before me. I truly believed that if I wanted to, I could have just walked right into the permagrass and onto a train. I could have dashed right up the steps of the Blue Comet and sped off into the wheaty night prairies with the Rocky Mountains looming just beyond.

Knowing I might be able to do this made me the happiest boy in the city of Cairo, even the state of Illinois. Me, Oscar Ogilvie Jr., in the dark safety of circling trains. Me, with my dad standing large beside me, working the central switches and the throttle, big as a car battery, that caused the trains to roar past, the signal lights to blink red and green, and made all things possible in the world.

CHAPTER 2

The voice of the wolf howled a thousand miles to the east in the fall of 1929. Something had happened in the city of New York. People called it the Crash. I did not know what had fallen or crashed, since I was only nine years old at the time.

Dad read the *Cairo Herald* aloud to me. "Millionaires are jumping out of skyscraper windows in despair," he reported. "Some of Wall Street's biggest tycoons have sold off their diamond shirt studs. Now they're peddling apples on the street corners."

"Why?" I asked.

"They lost all their money," said Dad.

The radio would not shut up about the crash.

When it was explained to me, the words fell about my ears like raindrops but did not bother to go in.

"Gambling like card sharks on the stock market!" Aunt Carmen was heard to say. "It's the work of the devil. Credit. Margin calls. Credit's what ruins lives! They're like fortune-tellers at the horse races, every last Wall Street tycoon!"

I did not ask what a card shark was, or margin calls for that matter. I had enough trouble on my hands. My problem was math. For me 1929 was the year of blinding math problems. When the teacher wrote the problems on the blackboard, my mind drifted everywhere, to the bugs on the window and the ticking of the wall clock. Our teacher never smacked us, but she did smack our desks plenty with her ruler. Each wrong answer got a *wham!* on the offending student's desk. I got a lot of whacks and whams that year and an F in arithmetic.

Dad tried to teach me a quick way to solve the problems. He had a secret shortcut for fractions, but I could not bring Dad's methods to class because the teacher did not approve of shortcuts.

In the year that followed the crash, my dad's tractor orders began to fall short of what they had been. There was talk about layoffs at John Deere. Dad was worried about being laid off his job if he didn't sell ten tractors a month.

Nineteen-thirty passed and things got worse. In the summer of 1931, Dad explained that all the money in the country had been sucked down the drain like soapsuds. President Hoover was no better than the Roman emperor Nero, violining away while Rome burned to a crisp. Money was no longer to be found in the pockets of the working people and farmers. Their savings were worthless.

Farm prices fell, and farmers stopped ordering tractors.

By August our menu changed. We dropped from beef to canned yams. From lamb chops we sank to Ham Stix. There were no more Muriel panetelas and no boxes from Rochester, New York. The catalog from Lionel still came in the mail, but now it tortured us with its pictures of the newest, sleekest trains.

One late-summer night, Dad found me deep in the pages of the catalog. I was looking at the "Brand-New Models for Christmas Giving!" page. There was a picture of a boy and his dad, pipe in mouth, glowing over their new trains on Christmas morning. Put a cigar where the pipe was, and it looked just like Dad and me.

Dad read the catalog advertisement over my shoulder. "She's a beauty, isn't she!" he whispered with a sigh. "The President." It was a new silver model, streamlined like a rocket ship with every car named after a different president. It cost three times more than any other train.

"Boy, it would be perfect on our layout, Dad! And look. They put a girl in the window of the observation car."

That was unusual. Lionel almost always featured boys, in, out, and on top of the model trains with their pipe-smoking dads. Never a girl.

"It's an expensive train. Maybe next year," said Dad.

"It's okay, Dad," I tried to assure him. "We've got plenty of trains!"

But even in our basement world, apart from the world above, Dad cracked his knuckles and frowned. He could not concentrate on the trains.

"Oscar," he said one evening, "they are going to take the house."

"House?" I asked. "What house?"

"Our house," said Dad, looking at the wall behind my head.

"But it's our house," I argued. "It's a free country. No one can take our house away."

"The house is mortgaged, Oscar," he answered. His eyes were open wide like the eyes of a sick man.

"What does that mean?"

"It means it's owned by the First National Bank of Cairo. The president of the bank, Simon Pettishanks, came here in his big Bentley when you were at school. The bank will repossess the house by the end of the week."

"But . . ." My mind raced in ridiculous circles.

"Aunt Carmen hasn't got an extra dime for a cup of coffee," he said. "There's nothing for it, Oscar. We're done."

"But where will we live?"

"They say there's work in California."

"Will we take our layout there? All our trains?"

"Oscar," he began, but he couldn't finish.

"Yes, Dad?"

His face answered me before he opened his mouth to speak. "The trains will be sold along with the house."

"What do you mean, sold?"

Dad winced as if I'd slapped him. "Oscar," he said, "if I don't have the extra cash from selling our trains, I'll become a bum. It means I sneak onto a freight train at night when it's on a siding and try not to get arrested by the railroad police. If I don't get arrested, I sleep in the cattle car with the hobos and tramps and get my wallet and shoes stolen. Sell the trains and I can buy a respectable ticket on the Rock Island Line and shave my face with Barbasol."

I didn't like his "I." I wanted to hear "we."

Dad continued, his voice gravelly: "I guess the bank president's son likes trains, Oscar. Pettishanks paid half price for 'em. It'll buy me a ticket to California, Oscar, and a month's money to live on while I try to find a job."

I did not wait to hear that I would be parked with Aunt Carmen and Willa Sue. My dad held out his arm to haul me in against his side, but I yelled like a boy on fire. I ran upstairs and out into the night, slamming the screen door. Pell-mell I hurtled into the dark, as if the cool spruces of Lucifer Street could stop the burning. I had no doubt the wolf was watching me, red-eyed, from a broken window of the Lucifer Fireworks ruins.

Like a storm looming behind the farthest trees, Dad's leaving waited in the wind before breaking over me. He wanted to work for John Deere, San Fernando Valley, but nobody knew what kind of work was to be had in California. Farming was different out there. Instead of alfalfa and wheat, they grew walnuts and oranges. "Out there" still overflowed with everything Californian, like Chinese food, palm trees, and Hollywood movie stars.

"Deere's got two branch offices out there," Dad said cheerfully. "I've just put in for a transfer." You had to look on the sunny side, he assured me. But his voice had no sunniness in it.

It was always my impression that kids live in a fenced pasture, heavily guarded by grown-ups. We were not allowed out of the fence. We were told what was going to happen but seldom why. If we were told why, it almost never made sense. Not the kind of sense that makes sense when you are eleven.

September 1, 1931, Mr. Pettishanks and his deputy took the keys to our house and ownership of the trains.

I listened through a basement window to Mr. Pettishanks speaking to an assistant.

"Pack the trains and the equipment in cotton wool, Frank," said Mr. Pettishanks to his deputy. "Get rid of this homemade layout. Get a couple of men to take it out and burn it. We need a clean basement to resell the house."

I wanted to pummel Mr. Pettishanks with my fists. I wanted to poke him in the nose and pour sugar in the gas tank of his Bentley saloon. But I did none of these things. My dad found me on my sheetless bed an hour later.

"Time to go, Oscar," he said. "Wash your face. You don't want Willa Sue asking you embarrassing questions about why your eyes are red."

Dad and I boarded the bus to Aunt Carmen's house with our two suitcases of clothes and a case of Ham Stix.

"I'm going to hide the Ham Stix behind that water tank in Carmen's basement," said my dad. "It'll be there for you, Oscar, when you can't swallow another bite of sardine casserole."

Dad wore his tie because he wanted to look sharp. The first leg of his trip was the 5:10 to Topeka.

"Don't drag it out, Oscar," said Aunt Carmen to my dad as he bent to say good-bye to me.

Dad squatted down. "I'll write," he whispered in my ear. "I'll write lots of letters, and when I get a good job out there"—his eyes were all blurry—"you'll come to me on the Golden State Limited. I'll send you tickets, and I'll meet you at the station in Los Angeles. I promise, Oscar."

"I have something for you, Dad," I whispered back.

"What?"

I had been holding it in my hand the whole time. Mr. Pettishanks had left it on the umbrella stand. Before he remembered where he left it, I had sneaked up and snatched it away, wrapping it in careful layers of toilet paper.

Dad unwrapped it. "Holy smokes, Oscar. It's a Macanudo. A rich man's panatela!" He held it to his heart. "I'll keep it safe, and when I see you again, I'll light it up!"

I waved him down the street, leaning as far out of the porch as I could, him walking backward, throwing kisses, and yelling, "The Golden State to Los Angeles, Oscar! Not long!" I held my fingers to my nose to smell the last of the Macanudo. I would never wash it away.

"Get busy with the kitchen chores, now, Oscar!"

said Aunt Carmen when she found me still staring out from the front porch railing into the empty street.

"I never did see a grown-up man cry before," remarked Willa Sue.

"Well, now you have," I snapped at her. But evidently the sting in my voice clearly said, *"Shut up, birdbrain!"*

"In this household, Oscar, we keep our fingers busy and our tongues polite," said Aunt Carmen. "Please wash your hands and get the smell of that disgusting cigar off them!"

She had gotten out a pound of blisteringly white margarine and had it waiting for me unwrapped in a bowl the moment Dad turned the corner of Fremont Street. The margarine, a snowy brick of soft fat, came wrapped in a waxy paper bag cheerfully labeled *Butterine*. In the middle of the fat was a tiny red button. I had to work that little scarlet dye pellet into the rest of the white lard, gradually diluting the intense red color until it spread out and turned the whole lump a revolting yellow.

"Dad buys butter," I said.

"That's exactly why he has gone and lost your house to the bank, young man," answered Aunt

Carmen. "Butter, trains, and cigars. It put him in the poorhouse! You'll find us much thriftier here!"

Nothing was the same after that.

When I came home from school, the supper casserole was all cooked. It sat on the stove in its green oven-proof baking dish. I was not allowed near the stove. "Boys cooking! That'll be the day!" said Aunt Carmen.

I went to bed when my homework was done, my feet scrubbed, and my prayers said in front of Aunt Carmen. As her footsteps receded down the hall, I got the stash of Lionel tickets out of my wallet that I had kept back from the sale of the train sets to Mr. Pettishanks.

I switched the Lionel Line Golden State ticket to the top. Of course it wouldn't so much as get me onto a streetcar, but I loved seeing the words printed in gold letters:

With the toy ticket in my hand, I could sleep.

• • •

Aunt Carmen made her living teaching piano and declamation at the wealthier people's houses after school hours. She had a regular route with once-a-week visits to each family.

I begged Aunt Carmen to leave me home. "I need to do my homework," I explained. She examined my latest report card. "You flunked arithmetic, Oscar," she said.

"I have trouble with long division and fractions."

"Well, that grade's simply going to have to improve," she said.

"If you let me stay home, I promise I will do my homework. *All* my homework. I will do better. Please, Aunt Carmen?" I asked.

Aunt Carmen didn't like being pleaded with. On the other hand, she didn't like me flunking out of arithmetic.

Willa Sue jumped up and down for attention. "We get key lime pie on Wednesdays at the Merriweathers' house," she said in a singsong voice, "and we almost always get a nice piece of chocolate cake from the Baxters' cook on Fridays." She twirled a coil of her hair in her fingers. "If Oscar comes along to lessons, Mama, maybe they won't give out so much pie and cake. Maybe we'll just get smaller slices, or maybe they'll even switch to Saltines crackers."

Aunt Carmen did not appear to share Willa Sue's worries about Saltines crackers. She frowned at my report card one more time and declared, "You are a boy of eleven, Oscar," in just the voice she'd have used if she were reading out the list of sick parishioners in church. "You will be responsible for at least a C-plus on your next report. You will watch the house. If I catch you reading a novel from the library or making any other kind of trouble, it's not going to be a pretty picture for you."

"Thank you, Aunt Carmen," I answered.

"The world is full of tramps and hobos," said Aunt Carmen. "They are desperate men who get off and on the trains. They wander around town in filthy clothing. They sleep in the alleyways and look for handouts wherever they can find them."

"Yes, ma'm," I said steadily.

"No one is allowed in the house. Do not talk to strangers. You may not use matches, waste electricity, or nibble on what is not yours to eat. Is that clear?"

"Yes, ma'am, and I can have the supper casserole

nice and hot when you get home if you let me light the oven!"

Aunt Carmen looked at me curiously out of her true blue eyes. I guessed that few people offered to do anything for Aunt Carmen because she herself finished doing everything before anyone else could think of it.

All she said to my offer was, "We'll see." Aunt Carmen put on her hat and her white cotton gloves, and down the street she marched to the bus stop, Willa Sue in one hand and her bag of sheet music and *Famous Speeches of Famous Men* in the other.

Over her shoulder, Willa Sue burbled, "I'm bob-bob-bobbing like a red-red robin because it's *Monday*! Monday is Betsy and Cyril Pettishanks day! They have cocoa with whipped cream! Sometimes marshmallows!"

"Pettishanks," I growled under my breath. The Pettishankses were among Aunt Carmen's piano and declamation clients. The Pettishanks boy was the one with my trains. Over the years, I had learned a few bad words on the playground at school. Now I strung them all together and said them out loud as soon as the bus had come and whisked Aunt Carmen and Willa Sue to River Heights, where the really big houses were.

I opened my book, *Arithmetic for the Modern Child,* and stared at the assignment. Fractions made me sleepy. I needed something to eat to keep me awake.

I padded carefully around Aunt Carmen's kitchen and looked in the larder. She didn't buy vanilla wafers or even cans of Vienna sausage the way I used to do at Rubin's Market. She had a larder full of black-eyed peas and canned codfish cakes. The only answer was pancakes. Aunt Carmen might not notice that one egg, a cup of milk, a dab of margarine, and some flour was missing.

I ate my pancakes with molasses because Aunt Carmen did not spend money on syrup. For cooking, Aunt Carmen used Spry, pure fat in a can, but I could not even look at the Spry without gagging and used a sparing amount of Butterine instead.

My fifth-grade teacher, Mrs. Olderby, just loved problems. Before tackling thirteen seventy-fourths divided by two-thirds, then multiplied by seven-eighths, I washed up the pan and my plate so sparkling clean that no one would ever know what I had been up to. The smell of fresh pancakes would be lost in the smell of warming turnip and condensed milk casserole.

After the first week of pancakes and fractions, I struggled to a D instead of an F on one of Mrs. Olderby's surprise quizzes. Watching Willa Sue and Aunt Carmen disappear on the number 17 bus and knowing my pancakes were ahead of me was as delicious as the hot pancakes themselves. I could not wait for this small adventure every afternoon. But then Mrs. Olderby suddenly jacked things up to decimals. Decimals in long division was a leap into the blackness of space. *Arithmetic for the Modern Child* contained the riddles of the Sphinx as far as I was concerned.

I looked at my homework:

Butcher Smith is selling pork at one dollar and fifty-one cents a pound and liver at two dollars and twenty-nine cents a pound. Butcher Jones is selling pork at two dollars and nine cents a pound and liver at ninety-nine cents a pound. Mrs. Brown wants two and a half pounds of pork and six pounds of liver. Which butcher should she buy from?

I was as lost as a child in the forest. Each problem was like trying to find the Northwest Passage, a route that did not exist. Dreaming out the window, I pictured butcher Smith and butcher Jones in their bloody aprons weighing meat. Who would want to eat that disgusting liver, anyway? Maybe Mrs. Brown liked one of the butchers better. Maybe butcher Smith winked at her across the hamburger meat. Who cared where she shopped, anyway? Not me!

I doubled my pancake recipe and worked on my homework from the glider on the front porch, using the daylight so as not to waste electric lights.

It was in the porch glider, on a brilliant October afternoon, that I sprawled with ten homework problems spread out on the seat around me.

If a rotor turns at the speed of 569,001.4562 an hour, how many turns will it make if its speed is reduced by .06%?

The nine problems that followed were much worse. My mind wandered to my trains. Where were they now? I closed my eyes and thought of my Blue Comet. Would I ever see it again? I knew I had as much chance of laying hands on my trains as flying to Mars.

"I can help you with that problem!" said a voice.

CHAPTER 3

I looked up. A man stood at the edge of the porch, looking in on my spread-out papers. He was wearing horn-rimmed glasses and a snap-brim cap. He did not appear to be in filthy clothes or in danger of arrest. He had a pleasant smile, and he smelled of Barbasol shaving cream, like my dad. The grandfather clock had dinged four o'clock. There was still an hour and a half of afternoon before Aunt Carmen and Willa Sue alighted from the bus.

"My name's Henry Applegate," the man said, taking off his cap politely. "I was a math teacher once." He replaced the cap and removed his glasses. "Raised three boys of my own! All grown," he added as he polished the lenses on a tattered but clean handkerchief. He was well spoken. That was a good sign. He was carrying a fat book. Another good sign. I didn't think tramps and hobos went around with heavy books under their arms.

He continued to introduce himself. "I taught algebra and geometry in the town high school of Searchlight, Texas. A year ago, Mr. Hoover's recession hit Texas badly. Everybody upped and went away. They closed the school. I lost my job, so I came up here to see if there was any work."

"Where do you live?" I asked.

"Got a room at the Y for twenty-five cents a day," was his answer.

"My dad lost his job, too," I said. "He went to California. He's going to work for John Deere out there. Soon as he gets his job, he's going to send me a ticket to go. He's going to meet me at the station in Los Angeles."

Mr. Applegate pointed to my paper with his pinky finger. He said, "The answer to the first question is five hundred sixty-eight thousand, six hundred sixty point oh five five, three times an hour. The answer to the second question is twenty million, four hundred ninety-six thousand, forty-one point oh nine, and the answer to the third question is six hundred million, nine hundred fifty thousand, four hundred seventy-eight point ten."

"Come again?" I said, pencil stub furiously writing.

Without effort he reeled off the answers a second time. "Once upon a time, I was even a mathematics tutor at the University of Texas," Mr. Applegate added by way of further explanation. I noticed him breathing in deeply and grinning. "Is that pancakes I smell?" he asked.

"Are you hungry?" I asked.

"I haven't eaten but a box of raisins in two days," said Mr. Applegate.

I retreated from the porch to the kitchen and made him a plate of pancakes all his own and covered them with molasses. I added to his lunch an apple, which was all I dared do for fear Aunt Carmen would notice something missing. I passed the plate out the window to him. When I turned away for a second, everything on Mr. Applegate's plate was gone, and he thanked me. In another five minutes, my homework was completely done.

"I am going to explain how to do it," said Mr. Applegate. "It's no good you just having the right answers. You have to know how to get them. Then we'll read a poem together."

A little comprehension flickered in my mind as Mr. Applegate showed me how to do the work. He was certainly a better teacher than Mrs. Olderby. It had never occurred to me that one teacher might be better than another. Teachers just were. You got them, one after another, the way you got shoes.

After math, Mr. Applegate opened *The Fireside Book of Poetry*. We read, "The boy stood on the burning deck . . ." Tears sprang into my eyes when the father and then the noble son die on a fiery ship in the midst of battle. Mr. Applegate passed me his handkerchief.

Mr. Applegate stayed outside the kitchen window for the first week. He did all the problems from afar. But when it rained, I could not bear to see him all wet and dripping. I asked him to come under the eaves and sit in the glider on the porch. I showed

him my postcards from Dad. He showed me how he did math in his head.

"You can train yourself, Oscar," he assured me. "Just use the palm of your hand instead of paper. That way you feel the numbers as you write them with your fingernail, but you can't see them. Makes you concentrate. You do that for a few weeks, and you'll start doing math in your head just like me!"

Each afternoon we lightened *Arithmetic for the Modern Child* with *The Fireside Book of Poetry*. One afternoon Mr. Applegate recited a poem called "O Captain! My Captain!"

"It has another dead father in it!" I complained, my lip trembling. "This time he's lying cold and dead on the deck!"

"Next time we will do a more uplifting poem," said Mr. Applegate.

"I don't *want* an uplifting poem!" I pleaded, serving him his plate of pancakes. "I want to turn myself into an arrow and fly to when I see my dad again."

Mr. Applegate's jaw dropped. "Now that is *very* interesting, Oscar," he said, actually suspending his forkful of pancakes, midair over his plate, on the way to his mouth.

"What is interesting?" I asked.

"Well most people would say I want to fly to *where,* not I want to fly to *when.* Flying to *when* is a very complicated mathematical concept. Perhaps only a handful of people on earth really understand it. It is the theory that time and place are one thing, not different things, discovered by Professor Einstein. He believes that time is like a river. All times are present at once along its banks. Everything future and everything past is happening right now at some point in that river. If we were strong enough and fast enough to get across the current, we could reverse course and go back around the last bend in the stream. We might see the Battle of Gettysburg and find Mr. Lincoln in the White House."

"We could?" I asked. "Then we could warn President Lincoln not to go out to the theater ever again!"

"Yes, we could, but if we did, every event ever after that would change, too. Who knows, Oscar? A new chain of history would fall into place like cogs turning on a billion sprockets. Herbert Hoover might not be our president today if Lincoln had not been assassinated. On the other hand, you and I might never have been born. It would be a foolish thing to go back in time and make changes. Not to mention, Oscar, that it would take a very fast rocket ship to go into the past. It would have to go so fast that it would disintegrate, and all its passengers would disintegrate with it."

"But how about forward? Could somebody like me go forward from now, just a little bit?" I asked. "Maybe just enough to find my dad?"

"Oh, forward is part of the concept, too, according to Professor Einstein," answered Mr. Applegate.

I answered Mr. Applegate with a puzzled look.

He explained more, if *explain* is the right word—I couldn't make sense of a single particle of his thinking. "Oscar, if you wanted to go into the future, you would have to travel more slowly than time itself. You would have to use the principle of negative velocity. Time would simply pass you by."

"Did Professor Einstein invent a way of doing it?" I asked.

"Alas, Oscar," answered Mr. Applegate, eating his pancakes now, "Professor Einstein is just a mathematician, not an inventor."

"There's always a catch," I said, and looked down at my first problem of the day.

A train leaves Station A at two p.m. It arrives in Station B three hours, four minutes, and thirty seconds later. Station B is 75.6 miles away from Station A. How fast is the train going?

"Who cares?" I moaned. "Who cares about the stupid train, the butchers, or liver prices?"

Every day Mr. Applegate ate with the speed of a hungry German shepherd. Every day he told me of his job-hunting progress. One week he raked leaves for the city park for twenty-five cents an hour. Another day he changed oil, lying on the floor under the cars in the Mobilgas garage. There was no regular work to be had.

The no-work stories frightened me. I was afraid the same thing was happening to my dad way out in California. Were Dad's cheerful postcards from this town and that just a mask over hopelessness? Were my dad's handkerchiefs tattered? Were there worry pouches sunk below his eyes, like Mr. Applegate's?

"Poetry gets you through the hardest times, Oscar. It's like a tonic," Mr. Applegate told me. "The world has forgotten poetry and how it heals the soul and body, too."

Mr. Applegate finished his pancakes, sat back in his chair, and out of his mouth came a stream of verses. It was a righteous theme, a moral Sunday-school kind of poem, but it had a kick to it and it made little goose bumps go down my back and lift the tiny hairs along my spine.

"I liked that one, Mr. Applegate!" I told him.

"It's a very famous one called 'If,' Oscar, and it was written by Rudyard Kipling. Come June, some unlucky kid in every school in America has to recite that chestnut on graduation day. Preachers love it; teachers love it! Weepy old army officers love it! But, darn it, when the blues come over me, I set myself right by reciting 'If.'"

"How can you remember so many lines of it?" I asked.

"There's a trick to learning things by heart. A secret code."

"Wow!" I said. "Could you teach me how to do it?"

"Nothing easier," said Mr. Applegate. He flipped

open *The Fireside Book of Poetry* to *K* for *Kipling*. I scanned the poem "If." With a pencil, Mr. Applegate made tiny red underlines on certain words in the first verse.

> If you can <u>keep</u> your head while all about you
>
> Are losing theirs and <u>blaming</u> it on you,
>
> If you can trust <u>yourself</u> when all men doubt you,
>
> But make <u>allowance</u> for their doubting too;
>
> If you <u>can</u> <u>wait</u> and not be tired by waiting,
>
> Or, being lied about, don't deal in <u>lies</u>,
>
> Or, being hated, don't give way to <u>hating</u>,
>
> And yet <u>don't</u> <u>look</u> <u>too</u> <u>good</u>, nor talk too wise . . .

"Now try to remember those key words in order," said Mr. Applegate.

"I can't possibly," I answered.

"The code works just the way 'Every Good Boy Does Fine' lets you remember the notes E, G, B, D, F in music," Mr. Applegate explained. "*Keep blaming yourself. Your allowance can wait. Lies and hating don't look too good!* Repeat it a couple of times, Oscar. Now can you recall your anchor words?"

The first verse of "If" flowed into my mind as

easily as "Twinkle, Twinkle, Little Star." Each afternoon Mr. Applegate and I got more of the poem down to memory.

One day we had run out of milk and eggs. I did not dare open a can of substitute turkey hash or even tinned cod cheeks in case Aunt Carmen found it missing. Then the idea came to me.

"You know what!" I said to Mr. Applegate. "There's a whole carton of Ham Stix hidden in the basement. My dad brought 'em from our house. I reckon those Ham Stix are legally mine." I made Mr. Applegate a nice hot Ham Stix sandwich on toast. He loved it. He said it gave him energy.

"Let me see your last test paper from Mrs. Olderby," he said. "Let's go over those answers."

We worked from three-thirty to five o'clock each day as the days grew short and cold. Aunt Carmen never questioned the missing pieces of bread. She never discovered about Dad's carton of Ham Stix behind the water tank.

Aunt Carmen did not exactly smile, nor did she offer any praise, but, lips pursed, she did say, "Oscar, your grades in arithmetic are more respectable than they were."

I beamed, but then Aunt Carmen soured it by tacking on, "It seems as if you have a better sense of numbers than your father. Your father is terrible with numbers and money. That's why he invested in those foolish trains and put himself in the poorhouse."

"I hope to get a B soon, ma'am," I allowed casually.

"Hard work will achieve it, Oscar," she said. "I hope your father is able to find some hard work for himself."

There had been nine postcards from my dad. Each one featured a picture of a new city in a new state. He had gone from Topeka to Little Rock, and from there to New Mexico, Arizona, then Fresno, California. There were no jobs, and I guessed his cash was beginning to run out. I had no address to write him at. I felt frozen in my half of our correspondence because I could not answer his cards.

My eyes prickled and nearly burst into embarrassing tears when I thought of him at dinner or in school. So instead I tried to imagine Los Angeles, City of Angels. In my mind's eye it was a city of temples and oranges, grander than any of the seven wonders of the ancient world. In the middle was the train station. In its fabulous halls my dad ran down a gold speckled marble platform to meet my train and melt the ice that cramped my heart.

On November 18, it sleeted all afternoon. I was afraid Mr. Applegate would not come in the bad weather, but he showed up all the same. It was too cold to sit outside on the glider. Nervously I looked at the clock. Still two hours before Aunt Carmen and Willa Sue would trundle up the street from the number 17 bus that pulled in at 5:51.

"We can sit inside for a while," I said. "I don't reckon they'll ever be the wiser."

I made Mr. Applegate a cup of cocoa to go with his Ham Stix sandwich. He was grateful. "I don't know what I'd do without you, Oscar," he said, wiping his mouth on his sleeve. "The food gives me strength. I've got a job tonight. Pays a dollar an hour. Shoveling slush and ice at some rich fellow's party up in River Heights. His driveway'll be full of fancy cars, and those folks don't like to slip and slide. One of the gardeners said the boss might even have a regular indoor job for me downtown. We'll see."

"What kind of job?" I asked.

But Mr. Applegate didn't know. His nose was running, and he blew it stuffily into his handkerchief.

"My shoes have holes," he explained nasally. "I caught a chill."

I wished I had even a dry pair of socks for Mr. Applegate. I had nothing to give him. Aunt Carmen had darned my socks five times, heel and toe, but they were too small for a grown man.

"I don't understand," I told him. "One day everything in the world was fine. Dad and I had lamb chops and ice cream. The farmers farmed and bought tractors and the teachers like you had jobs teaching, then suddenly, *bingo*! It was over. My dad is gone, and now we're lucky to have cold turnips for supper. How could it happen?"

"Greed," said Mr. Applegate. "Greedy Wall Street profiteers pushing their luck like high rollers betting right over the top. They stacked the stock market like a house of playing cards. They bet way over their heads, couldn't back up their spending, and it all came tumbling down."

I knew well enough from Our Lady of Sorrows Sunday School about greed. I wasn't sure if the money changers greased people's palms in the Temple, or the Tower of Babel, but it didn't matter. Sure as shooting, there were greaseballs and gamblers in the Bible, and their descendants had clearly been at work on Wall Street in October 1929.

Mr. Applegate and I solved the day's arithmetic problems, going through the hoops of show-your-work on each one. "You're not dreamin' about your train set, now, Oscar," Mr. Applegate prodded me gently whenever my eyes glazed over.

I looked up at the kitchen clock for a moment. It was exactly 4:15. I glanced out the window. "Holy mackerel!" I said. "There they are! Getting off the bus. They're early! You'll have to go out the back door!"

Mr. Applegate grabbed his tattered overcoat and vanished out of our kitchen like a rabbit in the night.

They noticed nothing amiss. Luckily the pot and cocoa cup were clean; the Wonder bread was tucked neatly in its wrapper in the bread box. The frying pan was hanging from its hook, brightly polished, all traces of Ham Stix gone, and the empty Ham Stix tin lay sunken beneath Aunt Carmen's coffee grounds in the very bottom of the trash barrel. The kitchen smelled of my lima bean casserole.

I looked up from my arithmetic. "You're early!" I said as calmly as I possibly could.

Aunt Carmen removed her hat. "The Merri-weathers have chicken pox," she announced as if chicken pox were a personal shortcoming. "They had a big yellow quarantine sign up, right next to the front door. Not a living soul is allowed in or out on account of the chicken pox. So that took care of Mary-Louise's 'Yankee Doodle' practice and the Patrick Henry speech that her brother was rehearsing. We went all the way out to East Cairo for nothing, and of course, I can't bill them for today."

"And no key lime pie, either," grumped Willa Sue. "I was all looking forward, and then here come the dumb yellow quarantine signs and no pie!"

There had been many a time that my dad had encouraged Aunt Carmen to get a telephone. "I'll call you up, Carmen, and pass the time of day with you!" Dad always said. "Then you can talk to me and not have to put up with the cigars!"

Aunt Carmen always pointed out that telephones, like electric trains, were expensive gadgets. They were a luxury for those who could afford them, not ordinary folks like us.

This did not stop me from saying to Aunt

Carmen, "If we had a telephone in the house, Mrs. Merriweather could have called—"

"What's this?" interrupted Willa Sue. She hefted *The Fireside Book of Poetry* over the table to Aunt Carmen. "This book's soaking wet!" Her voice began the singsong teasing of the playground. *"Oscar's left the ho-use! Oscar's been to the library in the ra-in and ruined the bo-ok, and he's in big tro-uble!"*

Aunt Carmen opened the clammy covers of *The Fireside Book of Poetry*. The book fell open where it had been bookmarked to Kipling's "If."

"Whose book might this be, Oscar?" asked Aunt Carmen.

"I don't know!" came tumbling out of my mouth. Willa Sue snorted from across the room.

Aunt Carmen flipped to the inside back cover, where the library glued its card envelope and stamped the return dates for each book as it was checked out. She tapped the column of stamped dates with her fingernail.

"Let's see," she said. "It seems this book was checked out today, November eighteenth, Oscar!"

My mind was flying in circles of explanations, but none were needed.

Aunt Carmen squinted again at the stack of date stamps. "Interesting!" she said. "This book, *The Fireside Book of Poetry,* has been checked out of the Cairo Public Library every week since early fall this year. Hmm! Not one checkout before that for ten years. Early fall is when I began leaving you alone in this house. This must be your favorite book, Oscar. 'If' must be your favorite poem!"

I shook my head no and nodded my head yes both at the same time. I could not control turning as red as a beetroot.

"Oscar," said Aunt Carmen, shutting the cover of the book, "did you leave this house without permission and go across town to the library today?"

"No, ma'am," I mumbled.

"In that case, explain this soaking wet book, checked out of the library today, please, Oscar!" she said, looking up at me with her true blue eyes.

CHAPTER 4

For all it mattered to Aunt Carmen, I
could have appendicitis and a broken leg, but she
would never leave me home alone again. She did not
trust me not to let riffraff into the house, endangering
myself, her bisque figurine collection, and everything else she owned in the world. "Steal, steal, steal!
Is what those tramps do," she told me during my
dressing-down. "And *you* let him *in,* Oscar! A common scallywag as if he were a man of the cloth!"

There was no telling Aunt Carmen that Mr.
Applegate was anything but a common scallywag.

As a punishment for letting a stranger into the
house, I had to write Rudyard Kipling's "If" ten

times in my notebook every night until Christmas. I was not alone. In the world of declamation, Rudyard Kipling's "If" was a hot number. It was Aunt Carmen's clients' hands-down first choice. Everyone wanted their son to recite it. Nearly all her unlucky students had to memorize all thirty-two lines of it, standing straight as ramrods while they spoke.

From that day forward, I had to come along to the piano and declamation lessons and do my homework in whatever house we happened to find ourselves spending the afternoon.

The bus took us to the wealthier parts of Cairo. The lessons brought us into the homes of families who could afford to have Aunt Carmen teach their little girls to play the "Moonlight Sonata" and their sons to give George Washington's Farewell. These were the children of our patricians, the Cairo Country Club families, every last one of them. They had cooks, gardeners, and driveways with cars in them. They possessed telephones without party lines and the telephones had whole rooms of their own. Their houses were furnished with glowing cherrywood antique cupboards and tables smelling of lemon-oil furniture polish. Their parlors contained thick oriental carpets and deeply upholstered easy chairs. The rich buttery smells from their kitchens were not the same as those that wafted out of Aunt Carmen's parsimonious oven.

Aunt Carmen kept one suspicious eye on me as I did my homework at strange dining tables and in unfamiliar inglenooks. If I tried to sink into one of the deep-as-your-elbow upholstered sofas, I was told to sit in a hard wooden chair instead.

Willa Sue brought her dolls to these lessons. She dressed and undressed them and took them for walks. She played endless games with the dolls. It embarrassed me to even be in the same room with her. Mothers and cooks thought Willa Sue had cherub lips just like Shirley Temple and found her charming. They gave Willa Sue choice slices of pie and cake. They looked at me and my arithmetic book as if I were a stray cat. Sometimes they'd give me a piece of gum, which Aunt Carmen made me spit out the moment they were not looking.

I endured. The only house I could not bear was the Pettishankses'. Betsy Pettishanks was a terrible little pianist. She burst into tears when Aunt Carmen made her start from the beginning every time she messed up on the second bar of the "Moonlight Sonata." Betsy was meant to be in a first-grade recital, and her mother wanted her to get the prize. Mrs. Pettishanks, in her fashionable dress with silk-covered buttons and linen collar, would drift into the living room just when Betsy was playing. She pretended to arrange and then rearrange vases of flowers or bowls of fruit. Encouragingly Mrs. Pettishanks hummed the "Moonlight Sonata" as if it might help Betsy through the trouble spots. Every time Betsy missed that second bar, Mrs. Pettishanks would startle a little as if a tooth hurt her. Aunt Carmen said privately that Betsy needed to be switched back to "Yankee Doodle" before advancing to the "Moonlight Sonata." Privately Aunt Carmen did not think Betsy had a snowball's chance on a griddle of getting a prize, but she said nothing about any of that to Mrs. Pettishanks.

On seeing me for the first time, Mrs. Pettishanks, wife of the train thief, had donated a pile of her son Cyril's cast-off clothing to Aunt Carmen for me to wear. "So much more personal than giving them to the church bazaar!" is what Mrs. Pettishanks had said to Aunt Carmen.

I was a shrimp. The push weight on the doctor's scale barely held at fifty pounds when I stood on it. Aunt Carmen took in Cyril's waistbands and turned up his sleeves and pant legs. I would grow into them one day. "In the meantime we don't have to take you down to Sears Roebuck for new clothes, and that's a plus for the household budget, young man." It was the greatest shame of my days to have to appear in front of Cyril Pettishanks dressed in his own hand-me-down clothes.

Cyril Pettishanks was in the fifth grade just like me, but I had never laid eyes on him before because he went to River Heights Academy instead of the public school. Cyril's father wanted Cyril to be on the debating team at Harvard one day. In order to prepare for this, Cyril had to memorize the great speeches of great men. According to Willa Sue, Mr. Pettishanks required a huge dose of Kipling, which, he said, "cleared the mind and soul."

Cyril was a handsome boy, if always a little damp. He had thick black eyelashes and a ruddy face. He was as bumptious as a Labrador retriever. Cyril wore a blue-and-red-striped tie because that was the River Heights Academy uniform, but the tie was knotted wildly and his shirt slewed out of his gray short pants.

In order to recite the Kipling, Cyril leaned forward against the back of a wing chair and rocked it. He took a deep breath, whipped a forelock of wavy black hair out of his face, and appeared to take the poem straight off the ceiling. "'If you can keep your head up when all around you / Are losing their heads and blaming it on you—'"

"'Keep your head,' not 'keep your head *up,*'" corrected Aunt Carmen. "And, Cyril, it's 'losing *theirs,*' not 'losing *their heads.*'"

"'If you can trust yourself when, when . . .'" he faltered.

"The words are not written on the ceiling, Cyril," said Aunt Carmen. "Look at your listeners. Gesture with one expressive hand as Kipling himself might have done. Picture Kipling in his pith helmet in the middle of the Indian jungle talking to the Punjabi natives! And Cyril, don't slouch. You wouldn't catch Mr. Rudyard Kipling slouching. Begin again, please."

I half listened to Cyril struggle with the words as I struggled with math. Dust motes spun in the afternoon light. Somewhere in this house were my trains. I wanted to see them. Where would they be? Probably in Cyril's room, wherever that was. I wanted to see my trains so badly that it hurt, so I muttered "Excuse me," and left my homework on the dining-room table. I ambled down the hall as if to go to the bathroom. The lavatory was tucked away in a little nook underneath the stairs. I opened the door and closed it firmly so that Aunt Carmen could hear it. I figured it would take Cyril a full twenty minutes to get through the first verse of "If."

Like a cat, I flew up the stairs and chanced a quick peek in each bedroom. Cyril's room turned out to be the last in the upstairs hallway. I opened the ten-foot-high mahogany door carefully, minimizing the squeak. A crimson Harvard banner graced the wall over the bed. On the bed were piled footballs, baseballs, phonograph records, and a football helmet with an *H* on the side. He had tossed swords, a catcher's mitt, and a bow and arrows in a pile on the floor. A catcher's mask, chest protector, and shin guards took up the chair. Two tennis racquets lay on the radiator under a cowboy hat. Cyril owned an embossed chrome six-gun set. The holsters hung on the bedpost with their fake ammunition belt, red jewels sparkling on the gunstocks. Dirty socks lay everywhere, but there were no trains. Not a sign of trains or layouts anywhere.

I turned to race downstairs again when I noticed one of Cyril's school notebooks on the bed. It was open to what seemed to be a book report. What I saw registered shock that dried my mouth. Cyril Pettishanks, born for Harvard, the First National Bank, and beyond, had flunked his fifth-grade book report. His handwriting was no better than a first-grader's.

Apply yourself, boy! the teacher had written over the failing grade. It gave me the spiny all-overs.

The next Monday it was only a matter of time before Cyril was waist deep in the quagmire of the poem. He had particular trouble with

> If you can dream—and not make dreams your master;
> If you can think—and not make thoughts your aim,
> If you can meet with Triumph and Disaster
> And treat those two impostors just the same . . .

Which he got sort of sideways with "if you can be the master of your dreams" and "greet those two impostors."

"It's 'meet with,' not 'meet *up* with,' Cyril," corrected Aunt Carmen. "And it's *treat,* not *greet!*" Cyril rocked the wing chair so hard it fell over sideways.

More patient than his sister, Betsy, Cyril reversed and started over and over and over again without complaint. He stood on one foot and then the other. He put his hands in his pockets, which made Aunt Carmen tell him to get his hands out of his pockets because Rudyard Kipling was an English gentleman in the jungle and English gentlemen never put their hands in their pockets when they were in the jungle. "Project your voice. Don't mumble, Cyril," she prompted. "Start at 'If you can make one heap of all your winnings.'"

I would have felt sorry for Cyril if it hadn't been that he owned my trains out of no fault of mine or virtue of his. Once again I went to the bathroom. I opened the door and closed it firmly as Cyril stumbled, saying, "If you can heap up all your winnings."

This time I flew through the kitchen and found the door to the basement. I flicked on the overhead light and dashed downstairs. Three entire suits of armor stood under the stairs; piles of furniture and numerous tarnished silver tea sets crammed the corners, but no trains. Along the wall, hundreds of old *National Geographics* had been stowed in sloppy stacks. There was a dressmaker's dummy tangled in the antlers of an enormous moose, but no sign of my trains, or even the boxes that might have contained them.

It was two weeks before Christmas that I had a chance to try the Pettishankses' attic. I waited for Cyril to bungle "If you can talk with crowds and keep your virtue, / Or walk with kings—nor lose the common touch," which he changed to "If you can talk to crowds and keep on talking."

"'Keep your virtue'! Cyril, not 'keep *on talking.*' Begin again, please," said Aunt Carmen.

I crept upstairs to the attic. Nothing in the attic but summer clothing in mothballed bags hanging everywhere. No trains. Where were they?

Downstairs, Cyril was having a particularly sticky time. I crept back into my homework position at the dining table. Today he only had gotten as far as "If you can force your heart and nerve and sinew," which he kept fouling up as "heart and *soul* and *sinew*."

"'Heart and nerve and sinew,' Cyril. *Nerve*, not *soul*. Start again with the beginning of that verse," said Aunt Carmen.

Cyril did it again. Again he said "heart and soul."

Mr. Pettishanks, Macanudo in hand, suddenly strolled into the room. He clipped off the tip of the cigar with a silver instrument from his pocket, lit it, and blew a long tail of azure smoke into the room.

"How are you doing, son?" he asked. "Have you got the Kipling poem by heart? Shouldn't take long! When I was your age, I used to memorize thirty lines of Shakespeare a night!"

I stopped in the middle of my history homework. Even Willa Sue went quiet and put her dolls down.

"Let's hear it, son," ordered Cyril's father. "And tuck in that shirt!"

Cyril began to sweat in great flowing beads. His ruddy face retreated to the color of unbaked bread. He inhaled as if for a high dive and sputtered, "'If you can keep your head on when all around you are losing their heads and blaming . . .'" Cyril lurched through as far as "mastering your dreams and thoughts." Then he braked on "meet up with Triumph and Disaster."

A curtain of silence descended on the room. I had actually been rooting for Cyril as he stumbled through the words. I couldn't help it. He was so afraid of his father, I thought he'd piss his pants. Without realizing it, I mouthed the words along with him, trying to get him to feel a rhyming code: *master-disaster, fools* and *tools*. I did not notice that Mr. Pettishanks's eyes were on me.

"What are you doing, boy?" he asked me, blowing a few rings of smoke my way.

"I'm . . . sir, I was just . . . reciting along with Cyril. I didn't mean any harm."

Aunt Carmen's eyes bored holes in me.

"Cyril, finish the poem!" ordered his father.

About you, doubt you; waiting and hating! My lips prepared to form each syllable for Cyril to follow half a beat later. But Cyril crumbled in a panic attack. I could almost hear his heart pound across the room. He turned and sprinted to the bathroom, where we all heard him sick-up loud and clear.

No one moved. Mr. Pettishanks tapped the ash

of his cigar into a green marble ashtray with two bronze Irish setters on it. "Can *you* finish that poem, boy?" he asked me.

Could I finish Kipling's "If"? I carried the master copy in the pocket of my coat, encoded for memory. *If you can . . . walk with kings* intruded on my dreams. *If you can bear to hear the truth you've spoken* came unwanted into the bathtub with me. At lunchtime, all two hundred and eighty-eight words of it were embedded in the very beans of my baked-bean sandwiches. Not only did I have to write the entire thing ten times a night; I had to listen to four other poor fools like Cyril battle through it five afternoons a week.

I stood up—in respect for either Mr. Pettishanks or Kipling, I did not know which.

"May I start at the beginning, sir?" I asked.

"Go ahead, boy!" answered Mr. Pettishanks. He propped a wing-tipped foot up on the seat of a dining chair and watched me like a buzzard. His eyes strayed to Aunt Carmen. Aunt Carmen sat motionless. I suddenly knew that she was, at that moment, a woman expecting execution. Her eyes sought only mine. In her face was equal measure of hope and fear, all bottled up in her wintery blue eyes.

In that instant I understood everything perfectly. Mr. Pettishanks wanted to know if his son's failure was Cyril's fault or Aunt Carmen's fault. If Mr. Pettishanks decided it was Aunt Carmen's fault that his son had flubbed the poem, she would be fired. If Aunt Carmen were fired by the Pettishankses, word would soon spread around the bridge tables in the River Heights Country Club that Aunt Carmen was a second-rate tutor, and she would lose all her River Heights clients. Mr. Pettishankses was not testing me. He was testing Aunt Carmen.

I did not read from the ceiling. I did not say "meet up with." I stood straight as a poker and looked Mr. Pettishanks in the eye. I did not stumble over *heap of all your winnings*. I gestured with my right hand as Kipling might have done, smack in the middle of the Indian jungle. The words flew from my mouth as perfect as a song. I sailed on through all the way to

> If you can fill the unforgiving minute
>> With sixty seconds' worth of distance run,
> Yours is the earth and everything that's in it,
>> And—which is more—you'll be a Man, my son!

without a single hesitation.

"Good," said Mr. Pettishanks, drawing deeply on his cigar. "You're a smart boy. I like smart boys. Here's bus fare and a dime for your trouble. Go down to my bank and give the night watchman this package. Tell'm to put it in the head teller's drawer."

He turned to go. Cyril had crept into the room, wiping his mouth on his shirt cuff, his attention on his father as a mouse might eye an owl.

"Learn it, son," Mr. Pettishanks ordered, his words boring holes into Cyril, "or you'll find yourself at military prep school for next term. You can bet your bottom dollar they'll drill some discipline into you starting at five o'clock in the morning!"

"Please, Father, no!" whimpered Cyril.

Mr. Pettishanks grabbed his son by the front of his sweaty shirt. He undid and retied Cyril's necktie and drew the knot up tight to Cyril's neck. In a spitting whisper that everyone in the room could hear, he said, "I was cum laude at Harvard. Your grandfather the same, and his father before him. My son is not going to be the first failure in this family. Do you hear me, Cyril?"

"Yes, sir," said Cyril, his eyes flicking on me.

"It's two weeks before Christmas. You get it by

the first week of the new year, or you'll find yourself in a cadet's uniform, drilling on the parade ground at the military prep. Think about it, son. Ice-water showers morning and night. The parade ground has flint chips on the track. They call it The Grinder. They make you do push-ups on it."

"Yes, sir," said Cyril. His eyes were dull.

His father released Cyril's shirt and gave his tie a small yank. "We can't have the public-school boys creeping up on ya and grabbing your slot at Harvard." Mr. Pettishanks eyed me and smiled without humor at his own joke.

Cyril tried his best to laugh. But when his father turned again to go, he snarled at me out of the side of his mouth, "You're a little worm, Ogilvie. I'll get you!"

"Do as Mr. Pettishanks asks, Oscar," said Aunt Carmen as if nothing had happened. "Do not linger. Take the number seventeen bus home when your errand is complete."

Out the front door I went, almost skipping with my sudden freedom. Free. Free as a sparrow in the sky for at least an hour. Unwatched and unremarked upon, I climbed aboard the streetcar and dropped my nickel fare into the slot just like all the free grown-up people. I might as well have joined life in Brazil. I turned my face upward to wherever God might be hiding. A tiny prayer of thanks blossomed in my heart, and I sent it skyward. Somehow I had pulled the lucky lever and got my dad instead of Mr. Pettishanks. Cyril would never learn that poem. With all his money and privilege, he was going to wind up in Missouri Military Prep, just over the river from Cairo. Everybody knew what went on there. Sometimes we could see them drill and hear them shouting on the wind. My dad said, "The Prep is supposed to be a school for troublesome boys, but it's really a school for the boys of troublesome dads. The Prep spits those boys out four years later as nasty little cadets."

The bus took twenty minutes to reach downtown Cairo and the intersection of Center Street and Washington Avenue. I alighted at the corner and went to the bronze filigreed doors of the bank. The First National was a heroic granite building. Ten fluted Greek columns held up the capital out in front. The bank's name was chiseled in the marble for all Cairo and the surrounding world to read.

Bankers' hours ended at three, but there was a

bell on the side of the double doors, and I rang it. Waiting in the cold afternoon for the night watchman, I turned to the right to one of the darkened display windows. Suddenly spotlights flared on. All that was in the Christmas display window came to life. There was a layout of twenty different trains in a Christmas landscape. The Blue Comet whizzed by. It was my Blue Comet. Mr. Pettishanks had it running lakeside on the South Shore Line.

Before I could even take it in, the night watchman opened the bank door and saluted me with a smile.

"Mr. Applegate!" I shouted.

CHAPTER 5

"Oscar," said Aunt Carmen after grace and before supper that evening, "you are excused from writing any further copies of Mr. Kipling's poem." She gave me a frosty smile.

"Oh, thank you, ma'am," I said. "That's a relief!" A grin, exactly like my dad's very own, widened across my face.

"You saved our bacon, Oscar," piped up Willie Sue.

Aunt Carmen frowned at Willa Sue and put her finger to her lips.

"Mama, that's what you said on the bus 'fore Oscar came home: 'Oscar Ogilvie Jr. certainly saved our bacon today.' I heard it with my own ears."

"Oscar," said Aunt Carmen, "you did remarkably well today."

"Thank you, ma'am. I sure know that poem by heart."

She asked me, "Did you know, Oscar, that the town of Cairo celebrates the Fourth of July with a fifth-grader reciting a speech from history? Each year one boy or girl is chosen from the schools. You might be the one selected if you practice. Perhaps we should prepare you for a few more recitations."

"It would certainly make Mama look good," said Willa Sue. "If you got to give the Fourth of July speech in front of the whole town, why, everybody'd know you were Mama's nephew! We'd get lots more jobs and a pay raise. 'Course you'd have to do it without messing up!"

"Hush, Willa Sue," said Aunt Carmen, but the cat was out of the bag.

"More speeches?" I asked. I stopped midspoon in my attack on the navy-bean-and-cod-cheek casserole. I knew all about the Fourth of July. Dad and I never missed the town picnic. We loved the band concerts. We marched in the parade. But when the hour came and some pasty-faced kid with glasses got up to deliver Woodrow Wilson's Fourteen Points, Dad said, "Let's get out while the getting's good!"

Aunt Carmen did not read the thoughts in my head. She plowed on informatively as she ate. "There's Theodore Roosevelt's Man in the Arena, of course. Then there's George Washington's Farewell. How about Abraham Lincoln's Gettysburg Address? That's a good one!" she said.

I felt the color drain from my cheeks and the sense from my mind. "Why don't I . . . look some of them over," I finally managed to suggest.

Famous Speeches of Famous Men was on my bedside table that night.

Aunt Carmen and I arrived at a bargain, without ever discussing a single detail of it out loud. She would allow me to visit my trains in the First National Bank in the afternoons after lessons. I would have Lincoln's Gettysburg Address committed to memory by the next July Fourth.

• • •

"Well, howdy!" said Mr. Applegate when I pounded on the doors of the bank. He flipped the alarm switch off and swung open the fifteen-foot-high bronze doors to let me in. He showed me how to slip the dead bolt bar that relocked the doors and flip the alarm back on again.

"All we need, Oscar," said Mr. Applegate, "is a false alarm. The cops'll come swarming down here, sirens blazing, and we'll be in trouble up to our keisters with old Pettishanks!"

Mr. Applegate made enough money from his new job as night watchman to buy a thermos bottle and hot chocolate to fill it. This we shared every afternoon before tackling the trains. In front of the massive lobby-wide layout was a small coin-operated box decorated with holly and red Christmas bows. The sign said

Young Savers —
Join the First National's Christmas Club!
Earn a dime for every dollar saved.
One dime runs the trains for five minutes!

I did not have to join the Christmas Club. Mr. Applegate knew how to run the trains for free by using a dime glued to a string over and over again. I kept the dime hung around my neck along with my Holy Name medal.

Mr. Pettishanks had placed my Blue Comet train on the South Shore Commuter Line. It ran the round-trip from South Bend to Chicago. I watched it run several loops before taking my eyes off it. No question it was my own train. On the side of the engine was a small scrape that my dad had carefully sanded and afterward repainted with cobalt-blue enamel. In its observation car were the two seats Dad and I had adjusted just so for perfect viewing when we would go down the Jersey Shore and see the great Atlantic Ocean for the first time. The windows had always been kept polished by my dad with a chamois cloth, and the nickel-plated side rods along the engine gleamed like silver.

Of course Mr. Pettishanks had replaced Dad's handmade layout with the official, expensive tunnels, mountains, and stations provided by Lionel trains and other makers. In the east stood Grand Central Terminal, New York. If you looked in the arched Plexiglas windows, you could see the tiny lights of the zodiac illuminating the vaulted ceilings. Dozens of tin people headed this way and that. Ten tracks went into Grand Central. Ten more led into and out of Dearborn Station, Chicago. Near it ran a Mississippi River of dimpled sapphire-blue glass with winking lights that rippled on a circuit beneath. To the west, the Rocky Mountains rose above everything, peaks covered with sparkling mica-flake snow. Nested in the mountains, Denver's Union Station shone like a treetop star above the rest of the country. The Rockies loomed a good five feet high above the base layout.

Beyond all the mountains and plains lay the country of my heart, California. Mr. Pettishanks's California layout contained tiny orange orchards made of seafoam dipped in flocking powder and expertly sculpted into trees. They were set on hills and in valleys surrounding the final terminus of the whole layout, the Los Angeles station, reproduced in tiny detail. I had never seen the terminal at Los Angeles in the Lionel Catalog. This one must have been invented by some expert in miniature buildings, probably costing an arm and a leg.

The sidewalk surrounding the station was crisscross yellow bricks, scored perfectly and scuffed to a real bricky surface. On the sidewalk near the front steps blinked a tiny red sign saying TAXIS. Three miniature checker cabs were gathered there. Each cab sported a Chiclet-size ON-OFF DUTY top light wired to its roof. When Mr. Applegate illuminated the station lights, the cabs waited for passengers with headlights and ON DUTY lights ablaze.

"Old man Pettishanks owns just about the entire stock of the Lionel catalog now," said Mr. Applegate. "He loves 'em. He comes in here every morning before the bank opens and runs 'em for an hour while he drinks his coffee and smokes his cigars. I don't know what he'll do when the Christmas season is over and the display has to come down."

"But I thought the trains were for his son, Cyril," I said in astonishment.

"Cyril!" said Mr. Applegate. He laughed heartily. "The old man swears he wouldn't let Cyril in the same room with these trains! Not on a bet! Cyril would try to have a train crash in five minutes. Cyril's a big galoot. He'd break the signals and put his foot through the windows in the stations."

• • •

There was snow coming on Christmas Eve afternoon. I took the mail out of the mailbox before I boarded the number 17 bus to the bank. Among the bills was a Christmas card addressed to me. In the corner Dad had put a real return address this time: *O. Ogilvie, Indian Grove Ranch, Reseda, California.* I ripped open the envelope. Good news! Dad had a job at last, even if it was picking oranges. Without comment, he had enclosed a dollar bill. Bad news, too. He had cut out a newspaper column from the *Farmers' Gazette:* "Deere Shuts Select Offices Nationwide."

I read on, heart sinking. John Deere had closed all of its California offices due to the recession in farming. Nonetheless, I put the dollar bill to my lips and kissed it because my dad's hand had earned and touched that dollar, two thousand miles away. I was not about to spend it anytime soon.

I shivered. The lowering gray sky darkened, and I ran out to catch the bus. At the bank, I banged on the door over the howl of the wind.

Mr. Applegate opened up. "Look at that darn snow!" he said. "It's coming down like the blizzard of '88. We might never get home, Oscar!"

Then there was a screeching sound. Behind Mr. Applegate, a Pennsylvania engine hung over a trestle bridge, its wheels spinning. The heavy engine dangled by a single coupling completely off a bridge over the blue-glass Mississippi River.

"It's going to crash!" I yelled. I threw my coat on a huge leather banker's chair and raced to rescue it before all five pounds of steel engine smashed the delicate river underneath.

"Wow, you're quick!" said Mr. Applegate. "Musta cost Old Man Pettishanks a small fortune to have that river custom-made. Imagine if we broke it! I'd owe him for five years indentured servitude!"

Mr. Applegate and I fixed the broken track bed under the engine just as Dad and I had done. Then we charged the engine stacks of all the rolling stock with smoke pellets.

"Everything set?" he asked with a grin.

"All aboard. Let 'em roll!" I answered. He pulled the throttle on the main controls, and all twenty-one trains raced around their tracks at daredevil speed. The lobby lights had been turned off, leaving two small all-night luminators, low glimmers behind the barred tellers' windows. Only the glowing lamps from the train stations and the small-town crossings glittered in the darkness of the bank's huge interior. Outside, Christmas Eve snow hurled itself against the thirty-foot bank windows. Drifts and eddies whirled under the street lights of Washington Avenue.

The lobby of the First National Bank of Cairo wasn't exactly as cozy as our basement in the old house on Lucifer Street, but it would have to do. For the next couple of weeks, whenever I visited my Blue Comet, for a few minutes now and then I felt as if I were home again, running our trains in our world below the world.

Tonight, when I rested my head sideways against the table near a bend in the tracks, the Golden State Limited on its way to California tootled past. From the club car, the tin man with the spectacles read his tin newspaper and the tin boy stared out at me. I wished a tiny Oscar could hop right onto the layout board and run into another world.

"Are you sleepy, Oscar?" Mr. Applegate asked.

"Not sleepy," I answered. "Just pretending."

"Pretending?" asked Mr. Applegate.

I was embarrassed to tell Mr. Applegate that

when I laid my head down on the layout there were moments when I truly believed I could be an inch tall and race up the verge of the station. In my dream, the papier-mâché rocks would suddenly be fieldstone. "My dad always used to ask me that same question," I said.

"You miss him," said Mr. Applegate.

A wave of sorrow swept over me, and I could not speak. I concentrated on the Happy Warrior as it emerged from a mountain tunnel, whistling and spewing out a delicate trail of white smoke.

"Mr. Applegate," I asked, "how long do you suppose it would take for one of these Lionel trains to run all the way from here in Cairo to Los Angeles, California?"

"Well, let's do the numbers, Oscar," said Mr. Applegate.

"If a train leaves Station A in the east vestibule and travels in about sixty seconds to Station B in the west lobby and the stations are, say, two hundred and twenty feet apart, how fast is the train going?"

I multiplied the distance times the speed. "About two point five miles an hour, give or take," I answered. "To go eighteen hundred miles at two and a half miles an hour would take seven hundred and twenty hours. Seven hundred and twenty hours is thirty days or one month. One month, give or take!"

"Very good," said Mr. Applegate. "But you are forgetting something!"

"What am I forgetting?" I asked.

"Professor Einstein's theory of relativity," said Mr. Applegate. "Now try it this way: If a train leaves Station A and travels in sixty seconds to Station B, and the stations are in actuality two thousand miles apart, roughly the distance from Chicago to Los Angeles, how fast will that train be going?"

I did the math in the palm of my hand. "Two thousand miles a minute and sixty minutes in an hour," I calculated. "That means the train is travelling a hundred and twenty thousand miles an hour!"

Mr. Applegate smiled. "As we know, any rocket ship going a hundred and twenty thousand miles an hour would just disintegrate from the heat. Even if the rocket ship was made of some amazing substance not yet invented, a passenger would die instantly from the g-forces," said Mr. Applegate.

"But how could it actually happen?" I asked.

Mr. Applegate sighed before he answered. "Einstein went just so far in his math, Oscar. But he didn't go far enough. He never considered negative velocity or time pockets."

"Time pockets?"

"Long story short, Oscar, if you were to sit in our make-believe rocket ship and it went east to west, you'd fly into tomorrow."

"I would?"

"Yes," said Mr. Applegate. "East to west, you would go into tomorrow, and if you kept going, you'd fly through a hundred tomorrows if you wanted."

"But California's west of here, and it's Pacific time, two hours behind us," I argued.

Mr. Applegate smiled. "You're forgetting the international date line, Oscar," he said. "No one knew how to contain the endlessness of time, so they made a seam around the surface of the world. But it isn't real. If your rocket ship flew over that date line three hundred sixty-five times, you'd be a year ahead. In no time at all, you could go ten years, even a hundred years into the future. Of course if you went west to east, you'd fly into yesterday and then a thousand yesterdays. To go forward into time that hasn't yet happened, you would have to slow down enough to plunge into a time pocket in Einstein's frozen river. You'd have to use negative velocity. Then you might do it."

Mr. Applegate's voice turned dreamy. "*Scientific American* claims that German scientists have been beavering away on all this in secret laboratories," he said. "They are working on time pockets. They call them *Zeithülsen*. They've built a primitive particle accelerator hidden underneath some mountain in the Black Forest. They're experimenting with snails and other mollusks, sending them backward and forward in time. Then they'll try it with mice and then chimpanzees. Eventually they will try to send a person back to 1914 and reverse the outcome of the Great War."

"Reverse the outcome of the war?" I asked. "The Germans lost the war. We beat the pants off them!"

"Yes, they did," said Mr. Applegate. "That's why they want to monkey with history. They want to change it so that they beat the pants off us. Who knows? They have very clever scientists in Germany."

Mr. Applegate smiled again, this time sadly.

"I could have been one of those scientists, Oscar. I could have run the American Negative Velocity Lab. There is none now, of course. American science doesn't believe in negative velocity."

"You could be head of the lab, Mr. Applegate?"

"I am an old man now, Oscar," said Mr. Applegate. "But when I was young and my mind was agile, I was the most promising graduate student at the University of Texas Department of Mathematics. I wrote my thesis on negative velocity theory, starting with Einstein's equation $E = MC^2$ and then improving on it and finishing it to its logical conclusion. I wanted to get a scholarship to Princeton to get my doctorate, Oscar! I wanted to change the world!"

Mr. Applegate swallowed very hard. He lifted both his empty hands as if something precious had dropped from them.

"Unfortunately," he went on, "no one in the Mathematics Department at Princeton could understand my paper. I didn't get my scholarship. I was a poor boy, so instead of becoming a world-famous professor like Mr. Einstein, I had to settle for being a high-school math teacher."

Mr. Applegate picked up a disabled freight engine

from one of the sidings, turned it over, and spun its wheels in the air.

I wandered to the other end of the bank lobby. I liked to watch the trains from different angles. The Blue Comet followed the curve of the lake along the Indiana dunes.

My favorite train, my dad's last birthday present to me, was leaving Beverly Shores Station heading east to Dune Park. Its whistle hailed me as if to say, "Hello, Oscar! I know you're there!" I pressed my face down on the bright green permagrass that sheathed the Nebraska plains to the west of Chicago and idly pretended that the oncoming express was absolutely real. The bells from Saint Savior's, down the street, chimed five o'clock. The Blue Comet looked huge, life-size, from my eye at track level. Suddenly, I saw movement at the far corner of the bank lobby.

I froze where I crouched, my head on the grassy layout, gazing down the tracks. Two men with silk stockings over their faces had come through the door without a sound. I hadn't locked the doors! I had forgotten to pull the bank's alarm switch back to the *on* position.

Snow swirled in after the men, bringing a jolt of cold air into the warm room. They crept up behind Mr. Applegate. I tried to shout, but before I could even open my mouth, one of the men whacked Mr. Applegate over the head with a club. All that followed happened in a kind of blur. I reckon the whole thing took only a minute or maybe two, but time itself slowed to a snail's crawl and I watched everything happen in the slowest of slow-motion pictures. I stood like a boy carved in stone until a shattering bang, much louder than any gunshot, made me leap out of my skin.

That's when one of the men saw me. He held the muzzle of a pistol straight out from his body. It was aimed directly between my eyes. In that exact moment, Mr. Applegate pulled off his blindfold. He rasped from the floor, "Jump, Oscar! Jump!"

Not five feet away, I saw a nail-bitten index finger settle over the gun's trigger. I smelled the oil from inside its barrel and panicked.

Facing the train layout at eye level, I tucked my chin, squeezed my eyes shut, and dived forward. Behind me somewhere, the gun went off like a firecracker.

I rocketed upward like a circus acrobat shot out of an air cannon and came down with a thump on my elbows and knees. I was a sitting duck and I knew it. The man with the gun would see me and shoot me in the tail. But I lay perfectly still on something horribly prickly and didn't move an eyelash. Somewhere nearby, a string of swear words echoed. Then clearly came the words, "Where the h——'s the d—— kid? He musta jumped into thin air!"

I closed my eyes tight as if doing that and holding my breath would make the men go away. Around me and over me rang a voice demanding, "Where's the kid? Where'd he go?" Furious, steaming words followed. "He was just here! Where the h—— did he go?"

"There's no kid. We're seeing things! Let's get out of here before the cops come."

Another shot rang out.

In front of me, a train rattled by, undisturbed, as if the shooting and yelling were part of another world. I had to breathe. My nostrils filled with a nauseating stink. The stink brought me back to our basement on Lucifer Street. I knew perfectly well what it was. . . . Kwik-Dri. Dad and I had made dozens of bushes and trees out of a cheap dried sponge called seafoam. This delicate foliage stank of the Kwik-Dri paint it had been dipped in. I was sunk in a row of toothpick-sharp Kwik-Dri seafoam shrubberies. Mr. Pettishanks had them too.

I lifted my head above the bushes just a hair, in order to see. The snow beneath my knees was not cold, as it was only mica-flake powder, which gave a nice sparkle. All I could see from my position was the underside of the tin bench next to me. On the slats was stamped **LIONEL COMPANY.** There was no mistaking where I was.

CHAPTER 6

I waited in silence for what seemed an eternity until I could stand the prickling seafoam no more. I rolled myself out, staggered to my feet, and thought about finding a telephone. The police had to be called, and an ambulance for Mr. Applegate, but where *was* Mr. Applegate? I frowned, trying to remember what had happened to him. Then I teetered and sank heavily down onto the bench. I was as exhausted as if I'd run ten miles. When I could get up, I stood and carefully walked a few steps. Beyond the very edges of the layout table, the lobby of the bank had vanished. In its place were the dunes of Indiana and beyond them Lake Michigan. The lake wind blew fiercely off the waves. It knifed through my sweater and whirled sand into my hair.

I snatched a handful of the snow that lay on a pine branch. It was cold. The pine branch was sticky with sap. My fingertips reddened. The flakes melted to cold water in my hand. The snow wasn't mica flakes at all. The bench on which I'd sat was not tin but stone and iron. Again I listened for pistols, thieves, bank noises. I heard nothing of the kind. Off the lake and into my lungs came the wind, salty and damp, a wind that could never happen inside the marble lobby of the First National Bank of Cairo.

A railroad depot loomed two stories above my head. The neat green trim around the station's main door was familiar. So was the white-and-emerald pattern of the tiles on the belvedere, yet I was sure I had never been here in my life, since I had never once in my eleven years left Cairo.

But this much was certain, I told myself. I was standing outside the Dune Park Station on the South Shore Line. How would I ever get home? Where was my world? I began to sweat into the cold wind and the fabric of my shirt. The station clock read 5:04.

A whistle shrilled suddenly and up roared the unmistakable grinding of iron couplings slamming to a stop. Puffing away on the tracks was the Blue Comet.

"The 5:04 local to Chicago!" said a voice on a loudspeaker.

I ran forward toward the steps of the train. I knew every side rail and nameplate. But this was no toy. It was a huge steel Blue Comet, the real train, but now on the Chicago track. No play smoke pellets poppled out of its stack. Instead, thick clouds of steam roiled into the sky. Black oil, gritty and hot, lined the crankpins and piston rods of the enormous iron wheels. The engineer's window was spangled with frost, and the whistle shrilled a deafening shriek.

"All aboard that's going aboard!" sang the conductor. The brass buttons on his uniform coat gleamed smartly in the doorway light. His red conductor's hat was beautiful to behold. I ran up the steps and found a seat in the first car, the Westphal.

"Tickets, please!" said the conductor.

Desperately I grabbed my wallet. It was a thin rubber one with gimp cowboy-style stitching, given out on saints' days by Our Lady of Sorrows Sunday School. The conductor did not take his eyes off it. No mistaking the Sacred Heart of Jesus embossed on one side. I riffled through the tickets bunched in their elastic band and pulled out the one that had come in the box with the Blue Comet set. In cobalt and silver letters was printed **BLUE COMET-JUNIOR PASS.**

I held my breath, waiting for the conductor to laugh and throw me off the train, but he placed the ticket into his time punch and slipped a receipt into the slot at the back of my seat.

"Chicago your final destination, son?" he asked.

Would my sudden plan work? I hardly dared to hope. Would I have to stay on this South Shore route only to loop back into the First Bank of Cairo and Aunt Carmen's cod-cheek casseroles? Or maybe . . . maybe this train would connect with other trains. I hardly dared to hope, but the answer fell out of me. "I'm going to California," I drawled easily. "My dad's going to meet my train at the station in Los Angeles."

The conductor nodded as if this were the most normal thing in the world. "Now you're gonna wanna change trains at Dearborn Station, Chicago, son," he said. "You'll have fourteen minutes. You're gonna wanna board the Golden State Limited. Go to track nine. There's a big sign, can't miss it, says Rock Island Line. She leaves at 7:09 on the dot."

The conductor went along to the next passenger. Outside, the engine whistle screamed and we pulled away. For a few minutes I rested my eyes on the rolling Indiana dunes on the right side of the car. Speeding right along, we passed between smut-belching factories.

A woman got on the train at the next station, Gary. She sat down next to me and smiled a little greeting. She reminded me of Mrs. Olderby.

"Young man?" she said after a few moments.

"Yes, ma'am?" I answered.

"I don't mean to pry, but you have some green substance all over your left cheek!"

I reached up to my face and brushed off a palmful of permagrass from where I'd pressed my cheek deep into the Nebraska plains on the bank's layout.

I didn't dare throw the grass leavings on the floor in case the woman disapproved and got me into trouble, so I squirreled it away in my shirt pocket. She got her hankie out of her handbag and dusted the rest off my face. "Now you look fine, dear heart," she said, and brought out some knitting.

I sank back onto the plush blue upholstery and drew breath deeply and painfully. I tried to remember the whole sequence of events in the bank. The stockings the men were wearing over their heads and faces had pushed their features into puddings of flesh. What had happened during the robbery was fading from me like wisps of skywriting. Did they take the masks off? Did they say their names? I closed my eyes and clamped my jaw shut in concentration. Recalling it was impossible, like catching a leaping fish with my fingers.

Outside the speeding Blue Comet's window, smut from the Gary, Indiana, smokestacks smudged out the sky. A dirty blizzard of ash fluttered by.

Deep breath, Oscar, I told myself. *Wiggle your lucky toes and say a few Hail Marys.* I did this with profound thanks to God, wherever He might be in this weird

world. Somehow I had been delivered into my father's train; more than that I did not know. But there was no mistaking where I was. Up ahead were the lights of an enormous city. Majestically they sparkled along the curved bank of Lake Michigan. Sure enough, I was headed northwest to Chicago and beyond.

The Golden State Limited was waiting, just as the conductor had said, on track nine. Only when I had scrambled aboard did I realize that I was still in a panic and a brain freeze. Clothes and shoes still on, I fell flat across the upper bunk of the nearest empty sleeping compartment. My sinuses throbbed. I was sure my head had swollen to the size of a melon and had filled with cotton wool. I could not exactly say I was in any pain. I saw no scrapes or bruises. But my body knew it had been through something very unnatural.

Somewhere on the Dearborn Station platform, the conductor blew his whistle sharply. Six cars ahead of mine, I heard the engine grind and chug to life. The couplings clanged, one iron mass slamming against another, as we lurched forward. Although I tried mightily, I could not lift my stone-heavy head from the pillow nor open my eyes. A porter marched down the aisle, rapping smartly on each compartment door. "Dinner in two sittings, ladieez and genl'men! First seating in thirrr-ty minutes! Thirrrr-ty minutes! Cocktails in the lounge." I was hungry. I could have eaten ten of Aunt Carmen's baked-bean sandwiches, but it didn't matter. In thirty seconds, sleep overpowered me.

I lay like a rag doll until the train shuddered to a stop sometime in the night. "Des Moines! Des Moines!" I heard the conductor yell. "All aboard the Golden State Limited!"

I drowsed back into a half dream. Suddenly, cold air rushed in as the door to my compartment flashed open, and somebody flung a suitcase onto the lower bunk. Whoever it was did not seem to know I was up there on bunk number two in the darkness. For one second I peered at him over the top of my railing. The man had put on blue-and-white-striped pajamas. He washed his face, brushed his teeth, and shaved, all the while singing off key, "I'm a rambling wreck from Georgia Tech, but a heck of an engineer!"

I did not wake again until the morning light was streaming through the window over my bunk. I opened my eyes fully. *Oscar, where in God's name are you? I asked myself. And how did you get here?* I had no idea.

If you could pinch your mind, I pinched mine. If you could pummel your brain into attention, I pounded on mine, but very little memory surfaced. There was a troll in a picture book I had when I was little. His trick was that you could see him only out of the corner of your eye; if you turned to look right at him, he disappeared. What had happened in the First National Bank was like trying to see that troll.

Lying on my back, I checked myself for bruises. There were none. I flexed my knees and ankles. All parts seemed to work. Carefully I slung my legs over the side of the bunk.

"Merry Christmas!" said the voice of last night's singer from beneath my feet. I withdrew my feet and curled back up into a ball on the bed. "Who are you?" I managed to ask.

"My name is Dutch. Who are you?" the voice asked. I could not continue to be alarmed. Dutch was not much of a singer, but his speaking voice was the most cheery and melodious I had ever heard.

I looked over the side of the bunk. His strong jaw managed a smile as warm as a June morning. I looked down on Dutch's full head of brown hair, parted on one side and combed into a little stack on the other. He wore thick horn-rimmed glasses and a Eureka College football sweater.

"My name is Oscar," I answered.

"Oscar, you traveling alone?"

"Yes, sir."

"Anyone meeting you at the other end?"

"Yes, sir, my dad." I answered automatically. "He's meeting me in Los Angeles, California." I did not tell Dutch that my dad had no idea where I was or that I didn't either.

"Good," said Dutch. He got out of his bunk, straightened up, and offered me his right hand. "Happy to meet you, Oscar," he said, grinning. "You're a fine-looking young fella!" He cocked his head when he talked. It was impossible not to smile back at him. "What are you gonna do in California?" he asked.

"I don't know," I admitted. "How about you?"

"I've got a girl out there!" said Dutch. "I'm on Christmas break from college. My girl asked me to come and meet her family. Imagine that! She leaned on her old man. He sent me a ticket and twenty bucks for the diner tab, or I'd never have been able to spring for it." Dutch chuckled. "Heck, I could eat all the way to California for five! With twenty bucks, I can eat like a king!"

I listened to Dutch's wonderful voice. He was clearly a young man of character. That was a good thing, because anyone would believe anything he might say. Just having him on the same train made me feel safe all over. I realized I was hungry. Dutch crinkled a smile at me. He stood as tall and broad-shouldered as any of the stars of western movies.

"I was sure you'd say you were heading for Hollywood," I told him. "You'd be a sure thing in the westerns, Mr. Dutch!"

He laughed. "Plain Dutch!" he answered. "You really think so, Oscar?"

"I think you'd be a big success, Dutch," I told him. "If you took your glasses off, that is!"

Dutch took the glasses off. "Now I don't look like a professor," he said, "but I can't see a thing!" He laughed and sat on his bunk to tie his shoes. "How about your dad? Is he in the movies?" he asked me.

"No," I answered sadly. "He's picking oranges. He lost his job selling tractors in Illinois. He used to work for John Deere, but they closed up their offices."

Dutch tapped his newly tied brogans. "Soon the banks'll close, and we'll all be in the soup," he said dryly. But I guessed that Dutch was what my dad called a natural-born optimist. No dark cloud could stay in his skies for more than a minute. He grinned and said to me, "Well, Oscar, you wash up and I'll meet you for breakfast in the diner. Is that a deal?"

"It's a deal," I answered, and jumped down from the bunk.

I brushed my teeth with a convenient Rock Island Line toothbrush provided for the passengers in a toiletry pack. I combed my hair with the Rock Island Line comb and washed my face with Rock Island Line linen.

The train was clipping at close to top speed, I figured. The car around me swayed and rocketed along the tracks. In the corridor, I looked out the window at the fleeing landscape. Dry and fallow winter fields sped beside us. Rows of gray earth followed perfectly parallel lines all the way to the horizon. Papery corn tassels blew in the wind. Once in a while a silo, lone and distant against the cold sky, broke the monotony. I made my way to the diner, which was two cars along toward the back of the train.

"Right here, young man," said the porter. He guided me to a seat and a crisp table setting, right across from Dutch. The cloth was thick white linen, spotless, with heavy silver cutlery on it. The napkin was folded like a hat with the Rock Island Line initials all entwined and a sprig of holly sitting in the top fold. The porter removed the napkin, snapped it twice, and tied it gently around my neck. He handed me the menu and smiled.

The diner car was filled with people. Had they somehow jumped on this train as I apparently had? Or had they come from their homes and driven to the train station in Fords and Plymouths the way all normal travelers do? There was no way for me to know, but no one seemed as lost and puzzled as I felt.

During breakfast, Dutch slipped deep into the sports pages of last night's late edition of the

Des Moines Register. He sipped his coffee happily. Suddenly he held up a knife. "They make the cutlery as big and heavy as they can," he said, "so light-fingered passengers don't lift the silver and squirrel it away in their pockets. What are you going to have for breakfast, cowboy?"

I looked at the menu. "I guess Cream of Wheat," I said lamely. It was the cheapest thing on the menu. I had only Dad's dollar in my pocket. I was so hungry, I could have eaten the plate itself.

Dutch made a face. "Do you like Cream of Wheat?" he asked.

"No, I hate it, but my aunt Carmen serves it every morning. I have to eat it, like it or not." I brought my dad's crumpled dollar bill out of my wallet and ironed it with my hand.

Dutch ordered us waffles with bacon, a luxury that never made it into Aunt Carmen's kitchen. "On me!" he said, eyeing my dollar bill.

"I never met anyone in my life who looked like a movie actor before," I said to Dutch.

"I don't know that they'd take me in Hollywood, cowboy," Dutch answered. "They'd probably say, 'Close but no cigar, buddy! Go back to the Middle

West, where you belong!'" He shot me a big grin and handed me the comics.

The waiter brought our waffles and bacon. I gobbled them up as if I were the starving boy from Armenia on the Our Lady of Sorrows alms box back home in Cairo.

Dutch had folded the front page of the newspaper and laid it on the table front page up. All at once I saw the headline. On the front page, my own picture stared back at me. I scanned the story quickly:

TRIPLE CRIME SPREE! CHRISTMAS EVE MASSACRE! MURDER! ROBBERY! KIDNAPPING!

DECEMBER 24, 1931—This evening at approximately 5:00 p.m. a gang of thugs broke into the First National Bank of Cairo, Illinois, at Washington Avenue and Center Street. The thieves shot the night watchman, Harold C. Applegate, who died instantly. The killers got away with $50,000 in cash from the vault. They left no clues. Nothing is known of the gang. Cairo Police say they believe that the thugs corralled a youngster who may have been visiting the bank after hours to view the extensive Christmas electric train set up in the lobby. The boy's aunt, Carmen S. Ogilvie of 41 Fremont Street, Cairo, reported the lad missing at 7:00 p.m. The boy's school bag and overcoat were found in the lobby. It is believed he may have been kidnapped because he was a witness to the crime. The boy's name is Oscar Ogilvie. He is 11 years old, with red hair and freckles. Anyone with any information leading to the arrest of the perpetrators should contact the police or Detective Gates of the FBI.

Mr. Applegate dead! It couldn't be true. There must be some mistake.

The picture was my school photograph, plaid shirt buttoned to the neck, my way-too-smiley smile, freckles clearly showing, and cowlick standing straight up on my head. Where did they get it? Guiltily I hoped Dutch wouldn't recognize me.

Dutch looked over the top of his sports section. Had he read the story? "Are you feeling top-notch, fella? If you don't mind my saying so, you look like a poke who's been dropped out of a ten-story window and lived to tell the tale."

"I do?"

Dutch told me, "Oscar, I've been a lifeguard for many years. I worked my way through college. Saved a ton of people from drowning. Your face is the color of a Sunday swimmer who swallowed half the pool."

"If I told you, you would never believe me," I said.

Dutch smiled. "Anybody headed for Hollywood better believe a heck of a lot more than your average John Doe. Try me," he said, and slurped his coffee.

The waiter came back with more coffee. Dutch tucked his napkin around his neck, just like mine. I wavered. I didn't really know anything about Dutch. After all, he was just a stranger on a train. "If you meet a man with a firm handshake and a steady eye, you can usually trust him," my dad had told me, "unless he's a politician. Then watch out." Dutch had looked me right in the eye, and his handshake had been as firm as a rock.

"You're not a politician, are you?" I asked Dutch.

"Not in a pig's ear!" said Dutch. "Now, tell me,

Oscar. Where did you come from, and how did you get on this train?"

What did I have to lose? "I am afraid I've died and am somewhere in heaven," I answered. The train whizzed around a curve, and I had to hold my plate steady. I had finished my waffles, but when I thought about it, I had never heard of dead people eating waffles. Plus, I was still hungry.

Dutch poured more syrup over his plate from a miniature syrup bottle labeled *Rock Island Line*. "Dead at eleven years old?" he said, without sounding as if he thought I was crazy. "Oscar, I can guarantee you that nothing of the kind has happened to you, unless we are both on an express train to heaven." He pointed out the window with his fork.

I looked out the diner car window. We were just careening past a station called East Libby. A farmer stood on the platform, hands in overall pockets, eyes dreaming down the track from a sun-wrinkled face. Next to him on the platform was a dusty old saddle. Then he was gone, spilled into the past. *Time and place,* I thought. *One and the same, according to Professor What's-his-name.* Another line of tracks split off and disappeared to the north through more miles of wintery corn fields, stalks bent and dry. The lonely silos on the horizon did not fit my idea of anything that might be heaven either.

"I can tell you one thing," said Dutch, tucking into his bacon. "East Libby, Kansas, is a mighty fine town, but East Libby sure isn't heaven." He wiped his mouth, signaled to the waiter, and ordered a second plate of waffles and more bacon for each of us. "I bet your story's a good one, Oscar," said Dutch. "You might as well tell me. We've got nearly two days to pass the time."

I pointed to the newspaper. He picked it up and read the lead article. Then he whistled loud as a hog caller. Dutch looked at the picture and then at me, and then at the picture and then at me again. "Is this true?" he asked.

"Yes, it's true."

"Holy mackerel, Oscar!" said Dutch. "Are you all right?"

"I think so," I answered. "I can't remember much. I know two men came into the bank all of a sudden. They whapped the night watchman, Mr. Applegate, over the head. Mr. Applegate was my best friend in the world. He's dead, and it's my fault for not locking the door and remembering to switch the alarm back on." Tears ran suddenly into my voice. "I loved Mr. Applegate, and it's all my fault!"

"Did you shoot Mr. Applegate?" Dutch asked.

"No."

"Those thugs would have come into the bank and robbed it, anyway, scout. You're not to blame."

I wasn't so sure. But I stopped sniffling.

"How did you get on this train, Oscar?" Dutch asked.

I could not tell Dutch I had jumped onto a model train layout. "I don't know, Dutch. I just know I dived forward, and next thing I knew I was in the station at Dune Park, Illinois. I jumped on the first train that came by and switched in Chicago at Dearborn Station to this train. Then I passed out."

Dutch took a pipe out of his pocket. He filled it, tamped it down, and lit it up. "Oscar," he said, "you're still gray as a mackerel. Whatever the heck happened to you, you're suffering from shock, same as a swimmer who nearly drowns. You need to sleep. Go back to the bunk and sleep it off."

I woke again in the evening as the train pulled into Denver and the conductor yelled, "All aboard!"

Dutch was not in the compartment. I lifted myself out of my bunk and stared for long, soothing minutes into the blackness of the passing land. We sped through a little town, its name on the station plate lost in darkness. I could see the closed-up storefronts reflected in a damp brick Main Street, lit only by one streetlamp as our train raced and rattled by. With my final wisps of memory of the bank robbery, the little town receded into the past, invisible and forgotten.

I found Dutch in the diner. "You look better, cowboy," he said. He had another newspaper folded beside him. "Sit yourself down. I've got news."

I brought out my same dollar and frowned again at the menu. I could perhaps afford a cheese sandwich, eating half now and saving half for breakfast.

"How about a steak, son?" asked Dutch.

"Oh, I couldn't pay for it, Dutch," I said.

"On me," said Dutch.

"Oh, boy!" I answered. "I haven't had a steak in two years."

The waiter brought me an orange Moxie. I hadn't drunk a Moxie since I could remember either. Aunt Carmen didn't believe in soda pop.

Dutch swirled the cherry in his old-fashioned in

a counterclockwise motion. He took a swallow and showed me the evening paper.

"We stopped in Denver for five minutes," he said. "There was a newsboy hawking papers on the platform."

In Dutch's hands was the evening-edition *Rocky Mountain News*. The paper was still cold to the touch. I could smell the ink.

CHRISTMAS EVE MASSACRE REWARD

A $5,000 reward has been offered by Cairo, Illinois, bank owner Simon C. Pettishanks for information leading to the capture of the murdering thieves-kidnappers who shot a guard, ran away with $50,000 cold cash, and apparently kidnapped a young boy who witnessed the crime. Roadblocks have been set up across three states, and trains are being searched. Any clues or information should be reported to the police or Detective Gates's desk at the Chicago FBI.

"That's the real stuff," said Dutch. "The FBI!"

"Wow!" I said. "Five thousand dollars!"

"It looks like payday for you, Oscar," said Dutch. "You'll be famous faster than me, that's for sure! Your dad will be able to buy the whole darn orange ranch."

I took a deep breath. "But, Dutch," I said, "I can't remember anything. I won't do any good to the police if I can't remember who did it! I think they said their names out loud. I think I saw their faces, too, but it's all like a dream I can't bring back." My voice squeaked.

"We'll work on it," said Dutch. "Let's go to the club car. First thing is, how about your pop? He's gonna be mighty worried about you when he sees in the papers that you've been kidnapped."

"I have no way to reach him," I said.

We sat across from each other in the club car in big easy chairs. Two ladies occupied the seats across from us, chattering away like magpies. The skylight windows of the Golden State streamliner opened above us to the stars and night sky.

"Oscar," said Dutch, "try to remember: How and where did you get on this train? Start at the beginning."

"It was Christmas Eve afternoon. Mr. Applegate let me into the bank to run the trains, same as always. Outside on Washington Avenue, it was snowing hard, blowing around like a blizzard. When I came into the bank, I saw an engine come off its track bed. It was a big one — those weigh almost five pounds! It was going to smash into this beautiful glass lake that Mr. Pettishanks had custom-made for the layout, see? We could have been in a peck of trouble if that lake had gotten smashed. That's why I got distracted and forgot the alarm system. . . ." I stopped. "That's no excuse . . . I know. . . ."

"Go on, Oscar," said Dutch. "Try to remember."

"I remember the bells of Saint Savior's Church down the street chiming out five o'clock 'cause I counted the five chimes. I put my head down right at track level and watched the Blue Comet pull out of Beverly Station on the South Shore Line. I like to do that . . . put my eye down at track level. It makes the trains look almost real!"

Dutch smiled at me encouragingly. "And then?" he said.

"Then it all goes blurry, Dutch. I saw 'em come into the bank, all right. They wore ladies' stockings on their faces. There was a huge bang, and the next thing I knew I was jumping on the local at Dune Park."

"Did you see the men enter the bank?"

"I must have."

"Would you know their faces again?"

"I don't know. I just remember one thing."

"And what was that, Oscar?" Dutch asked.

"Somebody yelled, 'Jump!'"

"Who, Oscar? Who?"

"It must have been Mr. Applegate. I can't remember anything else."

"Oscar," said Dutch, "I'd bet my bottom dollar those goons tied you up, stuffed you in a gunny sack, and dumped you in the trunk of their car. They must have scared the living pants off you. Somehow, Oscar, you gave 'em the slip in Dune Park. Somehow you got out of their getaway car and boarded a train. It's the only thing that makes sense."

"No, Dutch." I shook my head. "I jumped on this train," I said, "from another, bigger world. Maybe it's like something Mr. Applegate was trying to explain. I think it's called a time pocket. The Germans have a whole laboratory working on it."

"What?" Dutch asked.

"It's a very advanced scientific thing," I said. "I can't even do long division right, Dutch, so don't ask me!"

Dutch pulled on his pipe and blew out three perfect smoke rings. "I think you saw what a loaded gun can do, cowboy. You've got shell shock, sure as shootin'. Didja know, Oscar, what happened in the Great War? Our brave boys who fought the Huns in the trenches of France—know what happened to most of them? Well, sir, when they came home, half of 'em went down with shell shock. Oscar, dollars to doughnuts you saw point blank that Applegate fella get clocked. According to the paper, it wasn't pretty."

"When my dad wasn't there, Mr. Applegate near about saved my neck," I said sadly. "I guess I don't want to remember it or I might have nightmares for the rest of my life!"

"Oscar," said Dutch, "if you're going to get that five-thousand-dollar reward, you're gonna have to finger those goons."

"Don't I know it!" I answered. "Five thousand dollars would buy back our house, and my dad could come home from California."

"We'll take a break," said Dutch, and he took out his pipe and refilled it with Prince Albert special cut. "It'll come, Oscar. Like a deep-set splinter, it'll come out one way or another."

The train had begun an upward grade. I felt it in the slight slowing of our speed. We were in the mountain foothills on the eastern slope of the Rockies. It was too dark to see anything but the lights of a farmhouse here and there. Still, I could feel the earth lift beneath the train, and the *chicketa-chicketa* sound of the wheels on the tracks slowed its rhythm. *Dutch must be right,* I told myself. *Nobody can just jump onto a layout. There must be a sensible explanation for all this.* This was a real train with real waffles and real prairies outside.

I fell asleep and woke to find the starry lights of Albuquerque through my window. During my sleep I had dreamed of the Dune Park depot, where I had dashed onto the Blue Comet. Maybe I had been knocked unconscious by the thugs and thrown into the trunk of their car, only to escape at Dune Park. It made sense. But then suddenly I remembered, clear as day, that I had heard in the bank the Saint Savior's chimes at five o'clock and the Dune Park Station clock. The local to Chicago had been at 5:04 sharp. So the robbery had taken exactly four minutes start to finish from the time of the five-o'clock chimes of Saint Savior's. Four minutes exactly wasn't enough time for a robbery and a kidnapping. It was only enough time for something else, something physically impossible. I had jumped onto a toy train and escaped into some kind of time and space neverland.

Across from me in his comfortable seat, Dutch was scanning the paper again. He had it open to the Christmas Eve massacre story. Then it came to me. I glanced leftward to the two ladies in the seats beside us. They were deep in face-to-face conversation. The last time I saw them, they had been thumb-size and made of tin. So had Dutch. He was the metal man with the tin glasses reading his tin newspaper in my own train in my own basement. And I was the tin boy on the opposite seat, riding around and around forever through dark tunnels, over rivers, looping over the Rocky Mountains and back through Salt Lake City, staring out the window of the Golden State streamliner at another great big Oscar who might, this very minute, be peering in at me.

CHAPTER 7

Dutch and I left the train in Los Angeles. He had scribbled his real name and his girlfriend's telephone number on a piece of Rock Island Line stationery. I folded it into my wallet. "Now, listen here, cowboy," he said. "You better call that dad of yours, 'cause I don't see anybody here to meet you."

That moment I grabbed Dutch around his big swimmer's chest. "I can't call him, Dutch," I sobbed. "I don't have a telephone number for him!"

"I thought you said he'd meet you at the station. I thought it was all arranged!" said Dutch.

I continued to sob. I was ashamed, but I couldn't stop. "I've never used a public telephone in my life, Dutch! And I'll never see my dad again!"

Dutch slapped me gently on the back. "What's the name of the ranch he works at, Oscar?"

"Indian Grove."

"Well, sir, we'll just up and call 'em on the phone. If they don't answer, we'll send a telegram!"

"A telegram!"

"Western Union reaches a customer in two hours! I know. I used to be a Western Union delivery boy when I was a youngster like you."

Dutch did a lot of dialing and inquiring and waiting. At last he was put through to Indian Grove Ranch in Reseda. Suddenly Dutch dropped the phone as if it were a boiling-hot potato. "That thing gave me a shock like the electric chair!" said Dutch, holding his ear. Out of the phone's receiver had come the most deafening noise, like sheets of metal rattling. Then I could hear, "Hello? Hello? Indian Grove. Hello?"

Dutch picked the receiver up carefully. He asked for my dad, twice spelling the name. I watched Dutch frown at the telephone. He cupped his hand over the mouthpiece and whispered to me, "He doesn't work there anymore!"

"Can you find out where he went?" I asked, trembling.

"The fella doesn't speak a word of English," said Dutch. So Dutch talked very slowly and loud. "Where did Mr. Oscar Ogilvie go to? Where can I reach him?" Dutch repeated the question.

There was a long silence. Dutch at last nodded, hung up the phone, and tried Information again for another ranch in a place called Laguna Beach. He dropped more coins into the slot, and I could hear the sharp tone of a telephone ringing, heaven knows where.

Again Dutch asked for my dad, and again, after ten minutes of haggling and waiting, he was put off to another number.

My eyes stayed riveted to Dutch's face. He seemed to know that my heart was thudding away at a hundred beats a minute. Patiently and with his best smile, he dialed again. "Third one's the charm, cowboy!" he said.

The third number rang. I could actually hear an operator pick up the phone on the other end. "John Deere!" she said.

"Oscar Ogilvie, please, ma'am," said Dutch, his voice like honey in a spoon.

"Just a minute," said the disembodied lady. Dutch winked at me. Then the operator announced, "Mr. Ogilvie is out of town, sir. He's checking on equipment in Tarzana. He'll be back at his desk next week."

"Where in Tarzana can we call him?" asked Dutch.

"I don't know if I am authorized to tell you that, sir," said the voice.

My heart sank. Tarzana sounded as if it were in Africa. Could I walk the streets until I found him?

Dutch was not defeated. He introduced himself, first name and last. "Forgive me," he said, "but may I be so bold as to ask your name, please, ma'am?"

"Milly," came the reluctant answer. "Everybody calls me Milly, anyway."

"Well, Milly, it just so happens I have Mr. Ogilvie's son here right with me. Oscar Ogilvie, Junior. He has just arrived from Chicago on the train. He's only eleven years old and probably weighs forty-five pounds. It's Christmastime, and this boy needs his father bad. Can you help us out? We would so appreciate it."

I guessed Milly didn't have a chance against Dutch's friendly persuasion. I was right.

We stayed right by the telephone booth waiting for Milly to call us back. Several people wandered up and wanted to use the telephone. With his saddest grin, Dutch shook his head and said, "Medical emergency!" pointing to me. The people did not ask what kind of medical emergency and went away to find other pay phones. It took half an hour for Milly to call back.

Dutch picked up, and he just listened. Then he turned to me. "Milly's got your father on the other telephone, Oscar. For some reason, your dad thinks this whole thing is a hoax."

"It's not a hoax!" I sobbed, and the tears spurted out of my eyes all over again.

"Wait a minute," said Dutch, his hand on my shoulder comfortingly. "Okay! Your dad says if it's really you, you'll know right off where your mama died."

"Lucifer Fireworks plant. It was a lightning bolt did it," I said.

Dutch repeated this into the phone. Within thirty seconds, he had a new message. "It seems your dad is already in his truck flooring the pedal. Wait outside the station. He's got to get here from some lemon orchard in Tarzana. Most of it's dirt roads all the way down the coast till you hit downtown."

We walked to the hot-dog stand. "Three jobs in a week. Your dad sure moves fast!" said Dutch. "Sounds like he's got his feet on the ground, though." Dutch bought me a foot-long dog and a Hershey bar to go with it. We also got a morning *Los Angeles Times*. Even here in L.A., my face was plastered over the front page.

ANGRY BANKER DOUBLES REWARD FOR MASSACRE INFO! BOY STILL MISSING!

"Wow!" said Dutch. "Look at that! You've got ten thousand simoleons coming, cowboy, if you can remember who did the deed!"

This time I hugged Dutch in joy, not tears. "If you run into trouble," he told me, "just give me a buzz! My girl's old man owns a twenty-room house in Pasadena. That's where you'll find me!"

Swinging his suitcase in one hand, he waved.

With an athlete's gait, he swept through a high arch-
way. I waved back for as long as I could see him.
He waded through the crowds of people heading for trains, flagging down porters, and looking
for those they loved. I followed Dutch out to the
entrance of the station and watched him step off the
yellow-brick sidewalk into the world beyond. One
minute his foot was on the sidewalk; the next he
had disappeared and there was no trace of him to be
seen. I felt unbearably alone.

I sat on the steps outside the station and concentrated, hawklike, looking for my dad, not knowing
what color truck he had or the direction he might
come from. I hoped no one would recognize me
from the picture on the front page of the *Los Angeles
Times*.

The station had yellow stucco walls and towers
five stories high. They gleamed splendidly in the
brilliant sunshine. Palm trees clicked their fronds in
the breeze along the street outside. I ate my hot dog,
saving my Hershey bar for later, and watched traffic
passing by. The heat spiraled in waves off the side-
walks, although it was the day after Christmas. There
were an unusual number of soldiers and sailors passing

along the streets across from the station. I wondered why. You never saw soldiers in Cairo.

An hour passed. I read and reread the story in the paper about Mr. Pettishanks doubling the reward to $10,000, and the police being totally befuddled. I tried not to think about Mr. Applegate lying dead on the floor of the First National Bank of Cairo. *Try to remember, Oscar!* I told myself. *Try to remember the robbers' faces, their names. You know you know them.*

But nothing of the crooks' identity would come back to me.

Across the street, a newsboy was hawking the afternoon paper. I tried not looking every two minutes at the clock tower. I reminded myself that hot as it was in California, it was wintertime and dusk would come early.

The newsboy across the street was waving folded papers at passersby. "War fever! Read all about it! War fever!"

War fever? Some stupid war must have suddenly started that afternoon and knocked my story off the front pages. I wanted to know the latest scoop from Cairo. Had the thieves been caught? Had someone else collected the reward?

At that moment, a rust bucket of a truck drove up with *John Deere* written in script on the door.

"Dad!" I shouted. "Dad, over here! I'm here!"

My dad jumped out of the pickup. He hadn't heard me. He began searching, looking up and down the street. He focused on the station steps. He looked right at me, but he didn't seem to see me.

"Dad! I'm here! Right here!" I shouted. Again he didn't hear.

He took his cap off for a minute to scratch his head, and it was then I noticed that he was entirely bald. Bald! My dad always had a thick head of hair. Where did it go? He was wearing eyeglasses too. Where did they come from?

I ran down the steps to cross the street, but I could not step off the yellow-brick sidewalk that surrounded the station. I tried jumping and punching and turning myself sideways, but an invisible wall separated the crisscross brick pavement from the black asphalt. I tried another section farther down the sidewalk. I ran up and down trying to hurl myself into the street, but between me and the asphalt street was a barrier, see-through as a window but tough as steel. I was trapped.

Dad's eyes raked the area one more time, with his glasses and then without his glasses. I saw disappointment cloud his face. He raised both hands to his mouth and called, "Oscar? Oscar?" He saw no one he knew.

Disappointment overcame him, and he put his hand back on the door handle of the truck and began to open it. Panic quaked through me. My dad was going to leave. I would never see him again because I was pinned where he would never see or hear me.

"Dad!" I screamed. Could I turn my body into an arrow and burst through?

Dad lay the side of his head on the top of the steering wheel for just a moment. His shoulders hunched up, and he closed his eyes. Then he cleaned off his glasses and started the motor of the truck.

Then my eye caught a little red light flashing on the telephone pole above me. TAXI it said in white letters, exactly as in Mr. Pettishanks's station layout. Waiting at the curb, on the yellow-brick pavement, its ON DUTY top light illuminated, was a taxicab. I jumped inside it.

"Where to?" asked the driver. "Just across the street, please!" I said, and threw my only dollar bill onto the front seat. The driver shrugged. He rolled his eyes, as if to say, "Crazy!" but turned the ignition key and grabbed the wheel to back the cab up.

I fell back against the seat just as a hurricane wind pinned me into the upholstery and darkness descended. Thick-as-Jell-O air clogged my lungs. If there was any oxygen to be had, it was rubbery and as impossible to breathe as gas. The driver shifted the gears into reverse and turned the cab around. As the cabbie jerked forward, the blackness around me dawned to a milky light. I gulped for air. For a moment the whole world roared and clattered like a thousand marbles hitting a tin roof. I thought my eardrums would burst. It was the same noise, a hundred times louder, as had come through the telephone when Dutch dropped it.

"We're here, kid!" said the driver, and he stopped his meter at twenty-five cents. "Pay up — two bits!" he said lazily. Then suddenly he looked at me, and his eyes popped. "Get outta my cab, fella!" he said, and threw the cab into reverse.

I was already out in the sunlit street. I banged on the rear bed of the truck that my dad was just about to drive away. For some reason, my shoes had burst open, laces ripping. Aunt Carmen's careful stitching on the waistband of my pants had split. Miraculously I now filled the trousers out. A minute before, Cyril Pettishanks's shirt had hung on me like a pajama top. Now the buttons were tight. I grabbed the pant legs, tore through Aunt Carmen's hem stitching, and kicked them down. "Dad!" I shouted, tears of happiness choking my voice.

Dad braked. "Who in God's name are you, and what do you want banging on my truck like that?"

"Dad! It's me, Oscar!"

He only sort of recognized me. Suddenly a grin ringed his face so hard I thought his cheeks would give way. "Oscar!" he yelled. "Is that you? Is it you?"

"It's me!"

"Oscar! You're safe!" Dad jumped out of the cab. "You're not kidnapped anymore!" Then he just grabbed me. He gazed at me up and down, down and up, tears running down his face. He said not a word until he heaved a big sigh and mumbled, "God forgive me, son. I didn't know you. It's been ten years and, of course, you're a grown man now. Ten years, Oscar! Ten long years!" He was looking straight out and up at me, not downward as he always had.

"Ten years?" I asked.

"Almost to the day!" said my dad. "You've grown two feet! Where have you been? What did they do to you? Get in the truck and tell me!"

Dizzily I pulled myself onto the front seat of the pickup truck. Dad gunned the engine. He stole sideways glances at me as if he thought I might just disappear in a puff of smoke. I felt my head loll on my shoulders and fall.

It was morning before I opened my eyes. The air wafting through the open window was as sweet as any summer day in Illinois. The world smelled of citrus fruit. Birds sang in the trees outside the window. Dad was sitting on the foot of my bed. When I opened my eyes, he was staring into them.

"Is it really, really you, Oscar?" Dad asked.

"Of course it's me! What happened to your hair, Dad? Why are you wearing those glasses?"

"Hair? I lost it long ago. I've worn glasses eight years now."

"I've only been gone three days, Dad! Three days!"

"Oscar," said Dad. He frowned and offered me

a cup of coffee. "You disappeared ten years ago, after the kidnapping at the bank. They never caught them, those men. You were given up for dead! I was so miserable, I almost joined the navy and sailed away, but they wouldn't have me."

I wrinkled my nose at the coffee. "I'm not allowed to drink coffee, Dad," I said. "I'm just a kid!"

My father strained to understand me. There was no arguing with it. Dad was now a balding, middle-aged man. What was left of his hair was speckled with gray. I, on the other hand, filled the whole bed. I was bigger than he was. I was six feet tall instead of four feet, five inches. What happened?

A copy of *Life* magazine lay on the bedside table. I snatched it up. The date was December 1941. On the cover was a grinning, saluting new president of the United States, a man called Franklin Delano Roosevelt, standing on an aircraft carrier. I had never heard of him. America was apparently in the middle of a war.

I flexed my hand several times and studied the fingernails. They were mine, all right. I knew them well, and yet they were no longer the hands of a boy.

"You have grown into such a splendid young

man!" Dad whispered. "Handsome and strong and well spoken. I am so proud of you, Oscar!" Here he looked down and pounded his fist into his open hand like a ballplayer. "I promise never to leave you again, son."

"Dad," I answered, "you're stuck with me. I'm not going anywhere either."

I finally took the coffee, the first cup of my life, and eyes steadily on his, sipped at it. It was sweet, full of milk and sugar, and it did the trick. I got up and walked around as if this walking were new, like the coffee. Dad watched me with a hand ready in case I tipped over suddenly.

Gently, as if I were an injured kitten, he whispered to me, "What happened, Oscar? What did those goons do to you for these ten years? Where have you been?"

I couldn't answer his question. I kicked my big, new legs out. They seemed to work fine. There were no bruises on me, although I could swear I had been hit by a heavyweight boxer.

"Where are we, Dad?" I asked.

"We're in my rented room in Burbank, Oscar," he answered, his eyes following every move I made.

"Not much of a town. Just a little wink and blink on the map."

"I smell chop suey, Dad!"

Dad looked embarrassed. "I don't make much money yet, son. The room's over a Chinese restaurant."

I sat down and ate the eggs and biscuits that Dad served to me. "Oscar, tell me," he said. "No matter how bad they treated you, say it out. Tell me all ten years' worth."

"Dad?"

"Yes, Oscar."

"There is no *they*. I haven't been away ten years. It was three days, maybe, at the most. Three days ago, I got your Christmas card on Aunt Carmen's front porch. I opened it up and there was that dollar and the clipping about John Deere closing down all its California branch offices."

Dad wouldn't swallow this. He said, "Oscar, that was 1931, ten years back. Look at the magazine. Look at the paper. Look at you! You're twenty-one years old and six feet tall." Here he thrust a newspaper, the *Voice of the Valley,* onto my placemat. *December 27, 1941,* it read.

"Dad, I can't explain any of this."

"Well, start with the day I left Cairo," said my dad. He took out a cigar and offered one to me.

"Dad, I'm eleven years old and I don't smoke," I said, but I thanked him and put the cigar in my shirt pocket. I started at the beginning with Mrs. Olderby's fractions and Mr. Applegate appearing out of nowhere and helping me. I told him about the disastrous night of the forgotten wet library book and how that meant I had go on rounds with Aunt Carmen. I told him about "If" and Cyril and my trains being in the bank and my reciting the poem to Mr. Pettishanks.

Then I got to Christmas Eve. "Dad," I said, "I loved that man, Mr. Applegate. You being gone, Dad, he was all I had. He was sort of like a substitute you for me. He loved the trains. He helped me get by. And now he's dead and it was my fault. The whole thing was my fault for not locking the door and putting on the alarm." I began to cry into my hands.

"Not your fault, Oscar," said my dad. "Their fault." He called the thieves a name I didn't know he could say. "I know, son, that when terrible things get done to a person, sometimes they just blot the whole thing out. You must have grown up in some kind of prison those goons kept you in."

"I was on a train, Dad. Forty hours or so from Chicago to Los Angeles. I'm eleven years old. You've got to believe me."

My dad's face clouded in puzzlement. He said in his levelest Sunday voice, "Oscar, it's ten real years. This is 1941, not 1931. You were kidnapped and never found again. I counted every day of every month of every one of those years, and I cried into my pillow every night thinking of you being dead, being tied hand and foot in the trunk of someone's car!"

I was beginning to panic. Dad had to believe me—otherwise he'd think I'd lost my mind.

My dad finished his cigar and stubbed out the butt. I pulled out the one he'd given me and handed it back over to him to light for himself.

"What's this?" he said, spitting. "What's this green stuff on the end of this cigar?"

"Wait!" I shouted. "Dad, this proves it!" I turned out my shirt pocket, emptying it of a handful of bright-green grit, first into my hand and then into his. "Look!" I said. "You tell me what this is, Dad!"

He ran it through his fingers and smelled it. He made a face. "It's . . . it's that instant meadow grass!" he said. "Permagrass! We used to use it on our layout."

"Dad, before I jumped onto the layout, just before the crooks came into the bank, I had my face pressed down on Mr. Pettishanks's Great Plains. You know how I used to do that all the time at home. I got the grass all over the side of my face. Some old lady on the train made me clean it off! I put it in my pocket so as not to make a mess."

For the first time, my dad hesitated, and he narrowed his eyes, thinking. "I know this much," he said. "You're not in 1931 anymore, son. I sure as shootin' voted for Mr. Roosevelt in 1932 and 1936. President Roosevelt single-handedly pulled us through that terrible depression and set America on its feet again. These days movies are in color, Oscar! Sulfa drugs cure infections! And the best player in the American League is Joe DiMaggio! He hit forty-five home runs and stole seventy bases this season for the Yankees. Have you never heard of these things?"

"Never!" I answered. "But it doesn't matter now! Dad, we're rich," I said, rapping the table happily with the end of my spoon.

"Rich?"

"Yup. You can buy an orange ranch. We've got ten thousand dollars."

"What do you mean, Oscar? I've been working back up to mechanic all these ten years. I still only make fifty bucks a week," said Dad.

"Dad, Mr. Pettishanks offered a reward for anyone giving information leading to the arrest of the bank robbers. At first it was five thousand dollars, and now it's doubled to ten thousand! All I have to do is remember what the crooks looked like and what their names were. We'll be sitting pretty, Dad. We'll be thousandaires, if not millionaires! The reward was published in yesterday's *Los Angeles Times*. I saw it with my own eyes."

My dad shook his head. "Oscar. The reward has long expired. The cops won't catch 'em now. Everyone has forgotten the crime. We're in the middle of a war!"

"A war?"

"The Japanese attacked our navy at Pearl Harbor."

"Pearl Harbor? Where's that? The Japanese?"

Back home in Cairo, Mr. Kinoshura was Japanese.
Mr. Kinoshura ran the drugstore soda fountain.
"But the Japanese are nice people. What did they do
that for?" I asked.

"The whole state of California is paralyzed with
fear that the Japanese are coming our way and going
to bomb us next. Everybody's in a panic. All the
boys are joining up with the army and navy." Dad's
face changed expression. "Oh, no!" he said darkly.

"What *oh, no*?" I asked.

"Oscar, we'll have to be very careful. The army
is drafting every young man in the country. Just last
week the recruiters came out to the ranches looking
for Tip-Top Ranch's fruit pickers. The long arm
of Uncle Sam'll nab you for the army if we're not
careful!"

"But Dad, I'm eleven years old."

"Well," he said, "I believe in serving your country, but not if you're in the fifth grade." He looked at
me quizzically. He was considering the impossible.
I knew that much about my dad. He didn't want to
believe my story, but he knew that something about
me wasn't quite squared up.

Dad gave me an old shirt, a John Deere cap, and

a pair of his overalls to wear. They were still a little small, but way better than Cyril's old castoffs. Then he zipped up his jacket and took me to work with him. We drove from Burbank to Tarzana. There on the Tip-Top Citrus Ranch, we checked the engines of the machinery Dad had sold to them and to every farmer in the county. We changed the plugs on an old row picker and rotated its tires. Dad stood no more than five feet away from me as if someone might come and snatch me away from him. He introduced me to a passel of different workers coming on and off shift. They were from south of the border, but Dad seemed to speak a little of their lingo. None of them greeted me as if I were a kid, the way I was used to being talked to. I looked like a young man, as big as Dutch. I didn't want to be. I just wanted to be eleven.

"Blend in, Oscar," my dad warned me that afternoon when Mr. Tip-Top himself came to inspect the orange groves. "Blend in with the Mexican men. Pretend you can't speak English. Old Tip-Top won't notice you."

But Mr. Tip-Top did notice me. "Hey, freckles!" he said. "Come into my office. Take that hat off. You ain't no crop picker. I'm bound to report every able-bodied male on the premises who ain't got his army papers to the local draft board. Here they come! I hear their Jeep!"

"He's my son. He's just visiting!" said my dad.

"He better be registered somewhere!" said Mr. Tip-Top, and he strolled out to view his orchards.

Two soldiers in smartly pressed army khakis banged through the screen door, saluted, and walked confidently into the office. "We're looking for your orange pickers who've got their American citizenship, Mac!" they yelled at my dad. But the first thing they noticed was me. The sergeant couldn't take his eyes off me. He looked and looked as if he'd just spotted a chocolate malted with whipped cream and a cherry on top.

"I'm only eleven years old—don't look at me," I said.

"He really is only eleven," said my father. "He doesn't look it, but he is only in the fifth grade."

The soldiers winked at each other. "Trying to play cuckoo," said the one with sergeant's stripes on his sleeves. "That's one way to get out of the army! Some of 'em are putting blotting paper in their shoes.

Gives 'em a fever." He rolled his eyes. "Where ya from, fella?" he asked.

"Cairo, Illinois," I answered.

"Yeah? You register with your draft board back East?"

"Draft board? Heck no!" I said. "I'm in the fifth grade! I'm a junior altar boy at Our Lady of Sorrows Church in Cairo, Illinois."

"It's a long story," said my dad.

"I'll bet it is," said the sergeant. His companion, a corporal, took notes. The corporal grabbed me by the hand and pressed my fingers into a pad of stamp ink. Then he smacked them on a piece of paper. "We got 'em, Sarge," he said, and put my fingerprints in a file. "Go get drunk and kiss your girlfriend good-bye," he ordered. "We're comin' back Monday, noon sharp. Be ready. We're sending you out to kill a few Krauts, boy."

They trooped out as quickly as they had come.

"What are Krauts?" I asked my father.

"Germans," he answered. "We're at war with them, too, on the other side of the world."

"Germans! I thought we finished them off in the Great War!"

"They came back," said Dad. "They have a crazy leader called Hitler who started it all. Hitler and his Italian buddy, Mussolini. The Italians are in it, too! People are calling this the second of the world wars. Oscar, we've got to get you out of here!"

"Dad, I am eleven years old. Everything I told you is true."

"Oscar, we have to move fast, but I don't know where or how," said my dad. "I've half a mind to just skip town and disappear in the mountains of Montana till the war's over."

"Dad, I've got an idea," I said. "Let's sit in the truck and I'll tell you."

Unhappily my dad stumped back to the truck, frowning and staring into the middle distance as if somehow an answer lay there for him to see. He swung himself into the creaky leather front seat and shoved the gears into neutral, neither backing up nor going forward.

"Dad, I know you don't believe me about the train. About getting onto a Lionel train and coming out here," I began.

Something between a small chuckle and a sigh came out of his mouth, and he shook his head.

"They're going to suck you into that horrible war, Oscar," he said. "Unless we get out of here quick and disappear so they can't find us."

"Dad, would you hear me out? Please?"

"Shoot, Oscar." Dad worked his palm back and forth over the knob on the gear shift.

I tried to use my most sensible, logical voice. "We've got to find a train layout, Dad. If I did it once, maybe I can do it again."

"Do what again?" he asked.

"Get on it. Go through time. Go back to where I left off, in 1931. If I can do that . . . if I can finger those crooks, we'll be rich! This war will be ten years off in the future. You can come home to Cairo, and we'll get our old house and even our trains back. All I need is a Lionel layout, a good layout."

"But it's 1941, Oscar; 1931 is gone."

"No, it isn't, Dad. It's all right there on the river. All times are present at once. That's what Professor Einstein says."

"Professor who?"

"Dad, will you trust me? Will you help me find a layout and let me try? Because if I can go back to 1931 and you can come home to Cairo, none of this stuff will ever have happened. Not the Tip-Top Ranch or living here alone in a rented room for ten years and worrying about me."

My dad shook his head. "You can't get onto a Lionel train, Oscar," he said. "Be reasonable, son!"

"Dad, I did it before. I can do it again. I'll just put my head on the layout and convince myself that I'm as small as the little tin people on the platform. If I can make the trains look real size, I think I can do it. First thing when I get off, I'll go back into the bank. Somehow I'll remember the names and faces of those goons. They'll be arrested and Mr. Pettishanks'll give me ten thousand dollars. You can come back to stay. You'll even get all your hair back, Dad! At least for a while."

"Oscar . . ." said Dad.

"And you'll never have to leave me again."

Dad rubbed his eyes. "We're between a rock and a hard place, Oscar," he said sadly. "One way or t'other, I'm going to lose sight of you just when you came back to the land of the living. My boy has been returned to me in some kind of miracle, praise God, but Oscar," he went on in the same voice he used when he had to tell me he'd sold our trains,

"I hear the voice of the wolf howling in those hills out there."

"Dad, we have to find a train," I prompted him. "I have to at least try! If it doesn't work, we'll go disappear in Montana."

Dad brushed off his pants. He threw the truck into reverse.

"Trains," muttered Dad. "Expensive layouts. I don't know a living soul who could afford a layout these days."

"Let's go to a toy store," I said. "We don't have to buy a train. I just have to figure out how to jump onto one. But first I better get some little boy clothes. I can't go back in a man's work clothes."

We got in the truck and drove on old dirt roads through Santa Monica, alongside of the Pacific Ocean, then turned onto Wilshire Boulevard. We stopped at Bullock's boys' shop. Dad and I bought boy-size underwear, trousers, shirt, shoes, socks, and lined jacket and a zip bag to put them in. I threw in my Hershey bar for emergencies and my return Lionel ticket stub. Then we went on to Minshman's Toy Emporium, the biggest in the city.

As of December 7, 1941, Pearl Harbor Day itself,

Minshman's had discontinued their train layout. Everything in the window and upstairs, where the trains had run before, was inspired by the war— tanks, guns, and submarines. But they were all made of wood and cardboard. No metal. PLAY WITH OUR TANKS AND HELP WIN THE WAR! said a big sign. TEN PERCENT OF ALL MINSHMAN'S PROFITS GOES TO OUR BOYS IN UNIFORM!

We tried another toy store, and another. All were filled with miniature bombers and machine guns and junior-size army uniforms. There were destroyers, aircraft carriers, Jeeps, fighter planes, and antiaircraft guns. But no trains chugged around even a single loop of track. In the last toy store, the very helpful salesman told us that Lionel had suspended production for the duration of the fighting to save metal for the war effort. Dejectedly we sat in Dad's truck, the bag of boy's clothes between us on the seat.

"It's a dead end," said Dad. "Better to hightail you to a mountain hideaway until the war is over and the draft is done."

"Wait a minute!" I said. I took my rubber wallet out of my pocket and thumbed through it. Out of it I fished a worn piece of Rock Island Line stationery.

In faded, scrawled writing were the words, *If you ever need help, call me anytime, Oscar. Good luck!*

Under it was a Pasadena telephone number. My father looked at the signature. "Holy Mother of God!" he said. "Your Dutch fellow is a famous movie star. He's in a lot of westerns. You'll never get someone like that on the phone. He's too famous."

CHAPTER 8

A pleasant woman's voice answered the telephone. When I asked for Dutch by his real name, she began to laugh. "Oh, my goodness!" she said. "He's a movie star now. Ages ago he went to college with my daughter, Audrey. He came out from Des Moines at Christmas I think in '31, when they were sweethearts. We never saw him again. Audrey's married to a lawyer now. She lives in New York!"

"Do you know where to reach Dutch?" I asked, hope dropping into my shoes.

I could hear fingernails tapping the phone in concentration. "He'll never be listed in the telephone book. He's too famous," said the lady. "But just a minute. I think Audrey ran into him once in the Biltmore. He bought her a lemonade in the lounge. The studio keeps a room for him there when he's in town. If he's not on location, you may find him there. Good luck!"

At first the Biltmore Hotel operator did not want to put me through to Dutch. She took my name and left me hanging for five minutes. Suddenly a foreign man got on the line. "Biltmore lounge, may I help you?" he said. I asked for Dutch by his real name. Then I held my breath and prayed to every forgotten saint whose statue lined both walls of our church, not to mention Our Lady of Sorrows herself. Within a minute that wonderful voice was on the line.

"He'll never remember you," whispered my dad.

But he did.

"Remember you!" Dutch whooped into the line. "Oscar," he said, "you're the one who got me my first break in pictures. I auditioned till I was blue in the face and then bingo! I took off my glasses just like you said, and I got my first part. Oscar, are you hungry?"

"I'm always hungry, Dutch," I answered.

"Meet me in the Brown Derby restaurant for dinner in half an hour."

"Do you know where the Brown Derby is, Dad?" I asked when I hung up the phone.

"We can't go into the Brown Derby like this," said my dad. He had on his work clothes: a plaid shirt with a John Deere emblem on the pocket, stained workpants, and heavy boots.

We scrubbed up as best we could, but we still weren't very clean.

Nonetheless we rattled down to the Brown Derby in our fruit picker's truck and parked outside where fancy cars were all lined up as if for an auto show. Dad was too shy, so I gave Dutch's name to the head waiter, who sneered at us until suddenly a larger, even sunnier Dutch than I remembered strode in through the door. He wore a ten-gallon hat and sported a really good suntan. In order to see, he took his glasses out of a pocket and scanned the room. Then he smiled, spotting the cowlick on the top of my head, and put his glasses away. He had filled out and looked like the Prince of Hollywood. From his walk you could just tell that he knew it.

"How did you ever meet him?" asked my dad in a whisper.

"I told you, Dad. On the train!"

"Son of a gun! Still got that cowlick and freckles, pal!" Dutch said, and stuck his hand out to my dad and to me. "What a fine young man you've grown into, Oscar! I want to know . . . didja ever collect that reward?"

"You remember!" I blurted out.

"I felt like a heel leaving you at that station," said Dutch. "I got in that cab, and I said to myself, Dutch, you've done the lad a bum turn. You should go back and wait'll he finds his old man." Dutch's face had saddened at this memory, but he began to beam again and crowed, "But it looks like you were okay, cowboy!"

Dutch didn't turn a hair at how we were dressed, although the waiter gave us a once-over. We sat at a window table. Through it I could view Los Angeles, 1941, walking by. Women sauntered along in shorts and in trousers. You just didn't see that in Cairo, Illinois.

Dad was tongue-tied. He could hardly speak to anyone as famous as Dutch, but to me it didn't matter if Dutch were the president of the United States. He was still just Dutch. He ordered steaks all around.

"Did you ever remember what happened in the bank?" Dutch asked. "Did you ever get the names and faces of those robbers?"

"No," I said. "It's all just in the corner of my eye, but if I try to look at it, it goes up in smoke."

"Too bad," said Dutch, and he cocked his head with a grin on his face that I remembered from before.

"But only a few days have gone by," I said.

"Come again?" Dutch looked up.

Dad and Dutch exchanged glances.

"Dutch, I need your help," I said.

"If I can do it, Oscar, I will," said Dutch. The waiter whizzed the steaks out of the kitchen on sizzling pewter platters with baked potatoes and salads on the side. I hadn't had a meal like this since . . . since the train from Chicago. Since 1931. A couple of days ago.

"I need to find a train set, Dutch. A layout. A

big wonderful layout with lots of trains. Is there such a thing in Los Angeles?"

"Why, Oscar? If I may ask," asked Dutch.

My dad looked embarrassed and folded and refolded his napkin.

"Because I have to go back," I answered.

Dutch speared and swallowed several pieces of his steak before he answered. "Have you tried the toy stores? You could call 'em up. Somebody's gotta have a Lionel layout."

"On our way over here in Dad's truck," I said, "we stopped at the biggest toy stores in town. No train layouts. Everything's army tanks and fighter planes and submarines on display."

"It's the war," said my dad.

Dutch agreed. "The world's gone crazy since Pearl Harbor. Next thing you know, they'll round up every Japanese mother and child off the streets and drop 'em in a bob-wire paddock in the middle of Iowa." He signaled for the waiter and asked for drinks. "Every gimp-legged son of a gun in the state of California is going into the service. The army'll be after you soon, son," said Dutch. "They won't touch me because I'm so darn nearsighted, but you haven't got a leg to stand on with the draft board."

"Except that I'm eleven years old, and I came out here on a Lionel train," I said.

Dutch's eyebrows shot up, but he kept eating.

"You don't believe me," I said, hanging my head and looking at my plate. I shifted a piece of steak around in its sauce.

"I believe this, son," said Dutch, wiping his mouth on his napkin. "You had such a heck of a shock ten years back in that bank that you haven't come up for air. Where've you been all these years?" Dutch chopped his fork around inside his baked potato.

I studied the tablecloth. "This is everything I remember," I told him, looking him hard in the eye and not wavering. "Christmas Eve I was standing right at the west side of the bank's layout. The church bells rang five o'clock from up the street. I counted them. Five o'clock. Then everything's a blank until I saw someone's dirty finger pull the trigger of a gun aimed right at my head. I closed my eyes and jumped as hard and far as I could. I swear to God, Dutch. It felt like being shot out of a cannon.

I landed in a bunch of seafoam shrubbery painted to look like juniper. I was at Dune Park Station on the South Shore Line. The Blue Comet stopped at 5:04 and I got on."

Dutch frowned and swallowed some water. He ran his tongue over the back of his teeth, but he didn't say anything.

I reached in my pocket for my wallet suddenly. "Look," I said. "Here's the ticket I used to get to Chicago. It's got the conductor's punch mark right on the time, 5:04. It's not a fake, Dutch."

Dutch took the ticket and examined it. He passed it to my dad.

"These tickets, Oscar," said Dad, "they used to come in the Lionel boxes when I bought you a whole set."

"I know," I said. "I kept them all in my wallet after you sold the trains, Dad."

"Wait a minute," said Dutch. He turned to my father and stared at the ticket again, fingering the punch mark. "Oscar Senior," he asked, "you're an Illinois man, is that right?"

"Yes, sir," said my dad. "Born and raised."

"Well then, how long would you say it takes

to get onto a train in Dune Park and make a connection in Chicago for the Golden State Limited to California?"

My dad frowned. "Dune Park is give or take ninety minutes by rail from Chicago. So maybe an hour and forty minutes if you ran like a fool."

"Oscar," said Dutch. "You were on the Golden State. That train runs on the minute every night of the year, like clockwork. I know you were on the train 'cause so was I. As I remember, the newspapers confirm the robbery happened about five. You could have flown on wings, but you'd never have made the 7:09 Golden State at Dearborn Station unless you connected on the South Shore local. It leaves Dune Park at 5:04. That leaves four minutes for the whole robbery. No time to be bound and gagged. No time for you to be thrown in the trunk of a car. There's only one train a night to California, and I know you were on it 'cause I got on at Des Moines at midnight."

"But it was a real train," said my dad, puzzled.

"Indeed it was," Dutch agreed.

"Dutch," I said, "do you remember that phone

call you made? Do you remember that electric shock . . ."

"I'll never forget it!" said Dutch. "I couldn't hear out of that ear for a week afterward!"

"I think I know what that noise was," I said.

"What?" asked both Dad and Dutch, this time together.

"I think only the train and the station were in the year 1931. Whoever answered at Indian Grove Ranch was ten years down the line in the future. That's why there was that screaming noise."

"I've got it!" said Dutch suddenly. "I've *got* it!"

"What?" Dad and I asked together.

"I've got an idea." Dutch ordered ice cream sundaes all around. Then he excused himself to go to the lobby and make a telephone call.

The sun had set by the time we finished our ice cream and the men had drunk their coffee. "Joan's away, so Alma will let us in," Dutch had said mischievously when he returned to the table. "We can get in to see the Crawford layout. It's famous all over Hollywood. I should have thought of it before!"

"The Crawford layout?" my dad asked.

Dutch grinned with the pleasure of his discovery. "It's a model train layout as big as a small town, built right into the rock of the house's foundation. It even runs through a little tunnel into the garden outside. The layout belongs to Joan Crawford's little boy. He's only a baby, of course, so it's just for show. Joan's one of Hollywood's most glamorous dragon ladies. She has a temper like a faulty blast furnace. Lucky for us, she's away, and the house is rented to a nice director and his wife. We wouldn't want Joan to give us a guided tour!"

I did not want to ask who Joan Crawford was. My dad seemed to know. I knew no one in this ten-year-later world, not even the president or the biggest hitter in baseball.

Dutch's car, a brand-new Chrysler Thunderbolt, moved almost silently through the middle of town, its motor purring softly. We drove up into the hills northeast of Los Angeles, above the curve of the Pacific Ocean, sparkling in the night. Dad sat behind me in the backseat and hunched forward.

His hand never strayed from my shoulder, as if he could physically hold me back from the army, back from an unknown where he might never hear from me again.

"Where are we?" I asked.

"Leaving Santa Monica. Heading for Beverly Hills!" said Dutch. Beside us, front windows flashed by too quickly to take in very much. Each house contained a family that I glimpsed for a few seconds. In some windows I could see people having cocktails in their living rooms or dressing in their bedrooms. The lives inside the huge houses zipped by like pages of books I had not yet read.

Beverly Hills mansions came in every fancy building style a person could ever imagine. Dutch pointed out which house belonged to which famous actor. "Judy Garland lives there!" he said. "And Clark Gable over in that one."

Whoever they were, they all seemed to live in palm-ringed mansions with circular drives that looked as though they were groomed with a tooth-brush every morning.

"Who are these people?" I asked, but Dad told me to shush. He knew who they were, every single one of them. "I live a lonely life, Oscar," he said. "So I go to the movies all the time."

Dutch spun the wheel, and we turned up another amazing street lined with even bigger mansions. I peeked around the backs of them as we whizzed and zoomed past, catching glimpses of a jewel-like swimming pool, an arbor, a guesthouse. Many were set way back behind an alley of trees the way the houses of River Heights, Illinois, were hidden. Apparently, regular people were meant to know that the houses were there but not what the owners really had behind the trees.

Dutch's Thunderbolt churned up the streets of Beverly Hills. "Roy Rogers lives in that house right there!" he said. "Every boy in the world knows Roy Rogers!"

I had no idea whether Roy Rogers was a deep-sea diver or a banjo player.

I did know that there were certainly no cars like the Thunderbolt back in Cairo. Even Mr. Pettishanks's Bentley saloon looked old and stuffy compared to Dutch's racer. Ten years had passed since I had seen the world of cars and streets and people's clothes. Everything in 1941 looked so airplane-like, so modern. I wanted to squeeze my eyes shut, and at the same time I could not get enough of seeing how things were going to be one day.

We pulled into a driveway marked 426 North Bristol Avenue. "An Italian palace!" said Dad. Tiles covered everything, and vines grew up the side. Dutch turned to me. "Joan Crawford's away on location. She's lent her house to Hollywood's hottest ticket, Oscar," he said. "But he's no movie star. He's a little fat man, an English director. I'd give my right arm to be in his next picture, but he'll pick Cary Grant, sure as shootin'."

"Who is Cary Grant?" I asked, picturing old bearded President Grant, whose picture hung over Mrs. Olderby's desk.

Dutch didn't answer but got out and rang the doorbell. A lady came to the door. Dutch took off his hat and twirled it over his chest as he spoke. His strong features, the nearly center-parted hair, and the swimmer's chest had not changed, even if ten years had indeed passed without my knowing it. In the lamplight of the front door, he bobbed his head in the familiar "good evening, ma'am" gesture. Whoever the lady was, she was all smiles. For a moment she looked anxiously out at us in the car, and then Dutch beckoned us to come up the steps and into the house.

We sat down awkwardly in our workmen's clothes. The room was much too elegant for the likes of Dad and me. Along the walls were painted gold-leaf cabinets with copper fan-knobs. Many photographs of the famous Joan, autographed in big loopy writing, sat in fancy frames on the end tables and hung on the walls. Joan was a looker, no doubt about it. Raven waves of hair framed her perfect face. Lush-lashed, doelike eyes and full red lips smiled at me. I examined the many poses of Joan. She kneeled, hugging her two children. She sat, caressing a dog, or she rested her head against some handsome man's shirtfront. Joan Crawford of the Crawford layout was every bit a Hollywood star.

On the enormous glass table in front of me sat a ruby-glass ashtray as big as a hubcap. The objects and colors in this house were much too daring to make it through the Pettishankses' front door; nonetheless both houses had that mysterious smell of thick carpets, lemon-oil furniture polish, and butter piecrust from the kitchen. You never smelled those things in the houses of regular people.

The lady shook our hands and introduced herself. I was glad we just had friendly Alma instead of dragon-lady Joan. "You're here to see the Crawford layout?" she asked. Her voice was light and delicate, exactly like the upper-class ladies on the radio.

My father looked as if he had just met the angel Gabriel. "Who is she?" I whispered, as she led us into the bar.

"Darn it, Oscar, she's the wife of Hollywood's most successful director. He does suspense movies, like *Rebecca*—it won the Academy Award this year."

I shook my head. Alma offered us anything we wanted from the enormous chrome bar. I had to remind myself that I was grown-up now, voting age. I was old enough to ask for at least a beer. I had never drunk anything stronger than a sip of Communion wine in my life, and so I asked for a ginger soda.

"Miss Chow?" said Alma. Another person was sitting at the side of the room. She was a slim Asian woman in a red tunic and black trousers. "Miss Chow has come from China as my husband's personal assistant," said Alma. "Her homeland, as I'm sure you know, has been bombed and invaded by the Japanese." Alma prepared our drinks with a magician's swift touch, then served them with a worldly smile.

"My husband, Mr. H., will be home shortly," Alma explained to us. "But, Oscar, you will be quite the celebrity!"

"Who, me?" I asked.

"On the phone, Dutch told me about the bank robbers and the dead night watchman and the ten-thousand-dollar reward!"

I answered, "I can't remember any of it. The crooks are probably living it up in Mexico by this time."

"Mexico?" asked Dutch sharply. "Why Mexico, Oscar?"

"I don't know," I said, frowning and looking up from the floor. "I can't remember." At that moment I noticed that Miss Chow's eyes were riveted on me. Her gaze was as piercing as high-beam headlights on a moonless night. The sealed door in my mind had stood ajar for just a second and then closed again.

"Well, the Crawford layout is one of the big attractions of Hollywood," said Alma. "There's a bus for tourists who want to come and see the homes of the stars. Sometimes the bus stops outside and Miss

Crawford lets people in to see the gardens. That is, if she's in a good mood." Alma looked over at Dutch. "I don't know how to run the trains. Do you?"

My father nodded. "Do we ever!" he said.

"Well, I'm glad," answered Alma, standing and straightening her skirt. "The train is officially her son Christopher's. I wouldn't want anything to go wrong. Joan has such a terrible temper, you know! She'd probably break one of her cut-glass decanters over my head if anything happened to her son's trains."

Dad assured Alma that he had all the experience any miniature railroader could ever want and that the trains were perfectly safe in his hands. "I trust you!" said Alma to my dad. "You have such an honest face!"

She walked us to an elevator. I had never imagined that a private house could contain an elevator. It let us out two floors below. Alma flicked on the light switch. "Would you mind terribly, Oscar," Alma asked me, "if I tell my husband your peculiar story when he comes home? The one about the bank robbery?"

"No," I said. "I don't mind at all."

She gave a sweet smile to me and my dad. "My

husband collects crime stories. He just loves the true ones, and I know he'll want to hear yours!"

The ceiling light revealed a layout far superior even to Mr. Pettishanks's and certainly to our old one in the basement on Lucifer Street. There were forklifts and coal ramps and barrel loaders. There was an entire Union Pacific freight with sixty cars. I stared openmouthed. Gone were the simple work trains and steam engines. The new additions to the Lionel line of the past ten years were like dream trains. Along with old favorites were new torpedo-shaped streamliner engines of great power. The Commodore Vanderbilt, the Hudson, and the Hiawatha, with a brilliant gold eagle on its engine, roared through the tunnels. The Flying Yankee flashed around its tracks. Floodlights and gondolas abounded. My dad was not prepared for the Crawford layout. When he saw the trains, tears brimmed in his eyes and broke his voice. "I haven't looked at a train set in ten years," he said shakily.

Dutch gave him a friendly swat between the shoulder blades. "Your son is alive and well, Oscar Senior," he said. "Thank your lucky stars and be glad!"

My dad smiled and wiped his eyes. "The sight of the trains knocks years off me!" he agreed.

Unlike my dad, I was all business. I noticed that Grand Central Terminal, New York City, was a slightly bigger model than Mr. Pettishanks's Grand Central. It connected with the Southern Railway and the route up to Buffalo as well.

No papier-mâché mountains for Christopher Crawford. His Rocky Mountains were solid granite. They had been chiseled and created out of the natural stone formations that lay under the foundation of the house. Pikes Peak rose to enormous heights. The mountain passes and cliffs were all artificially carved but appeared real as real could be. Dad explained that Christopher's Los Angeles station was the new one I had seen myself, Union Station. It was amazing. Outside it, ruby-red outdoor lamps were held aloft by goddesses. Ten trains ran in and out of its mammoth roundhouse.

The jewel of the layout, however, was a Hell Gate Bridge. This had always been the most elaborate structure that Lionel carried and the most expensive. Even Mr. Pettishanks had not owned a Hell Gate Bridge. It was a magnificent work of

engineering, a suspension bridge every bit as impressive as a real bridge a hundred times its size.

I found a spot where the Union Pacific sped out of a tunnel, crossing the tracks of the Atchison, Topeka and Santa Fe. The smaller train had stopped at a signal for the bigger train to pass. Holding my bag of new boys' clothes tightly in my hand, I lay my cheek on the scratchy fake grass of the layout board. Hard as I could, I let my eye imagine me right up to the cowcatcher on the giant life-size engine. I pictured the coals in between the tracks as big as baseballs in my hands. I could almost hear the patter of my feet on the yellow tile floor of the fancy new L.A. station. Dutch followed me with his eyes.

Could I do it? Everything seemed right. Everything but one part. Could I leave my dad?

My dad whispered, "Do you think you can do it, Oscar? Do you think you can?"

I answered, "You'll know right away, Dad. If I can do it, I'll just be gone, like that."

My dad held me in his arms for a long minute. Then he swung me away and looked into my face. He ran his hand anxiously over where his hair had once grown thick and black. He said nothing for a moment, but then nodded. "Good-bye, Oscar," he whispered.

"Good-bye, Dad!" I said in my deep man's voice, which nonetheless cracked as I said it.

My dad couldn't watch. He turned his back. Dutch thumped me between the shoulders. I felt the pull of my dad like a lifeline to a ship. But I was going to make us rich. I smiled through the tears that had filled my eyes.

Suddenly in his biggest football-field voice, Dutch yelled, "Go, Oscar! Go!" and I did, leaping into the layout with all my might, leaving my heart behind.

CHAPTER 9

When I came to, the light fixture above me was inscribed MERCY HOSPITAL, LOS ANGELES COUNTY. The emergency room smelled of disinfectant and canned soup. Sympathetic eyes and expert fingers examined my cut-up face.

"Hello," said a capable voice, "I'm Nurse Washington." It was nine o'clock at night, and she was tired; I could see that by her red-rimmed eyes. She peered at my eyes critically, under the blinding examination light.

"No concussion," she announced. Then she shook her curls and shifted her chair back to her desk with a waxy squeak on the linoleum floor.

This time I had no loss of memory. I could picture every awful detail. My bag had flown out of my hand and landed heavily in front of L.A.'s new Union Station, just missing the beautiful stucco towers. I'd cracked my skull on the crest of Christopher Crawford's bona-fide granite Pikes Peak, which was sculpted into a Matterhorn of a point. Bouncing off it, I smashed into Denver's Union Station with its tiny panes of real glass, all of which splintered into a thousand shards, spearing my face. My right foot had hooked the girders of the Hell Gate Bridge, over the East Colorado River, smashing the bridge and my knee beyond where I wanted to look at either. But why? Why had it gone so terribly wrong? What was different?

I tried to stop sniffling and shaking like an eleven-year-old. "It will take a month of Sundays to get the glass shards out of your cheeks, young man," Nurse Washington said.

"Are you going to have to use a lance or anything?" I asked.

"Tweezers will do," she answered. "You are very sensitive for a young man of twenty-one," she said, picking the word *sensitive* instead of calling me an outright chicken. "What do you do for a living?"

Before I could answer, "Fifth-grader, altar boy in Our Lady of Sorrows, Cairo, Illinois," my dad said, "I'm afraid he's a private in the United States Army as of this coming Monday."

"I hope they send you somewhere safe," said the nurse, grim-voiced. "Not that there's anywhere safe in a war." She made me lie down on a gurney under an even brighter light and wheeled up next to me with her tweezers at the ready. "How exactly did this happen?" she asked.

"I fell," I said. "I fell right into an electric train layout. Pikes Peak was real rock. The Denver station model had real glass in the windows."

"My stars!" said Nurse Washington. "If you were breathing beer fumes at me like so many of them do, I wouldn't believe you, but there is something so innocent about you."

I had to act grown-up, whatever that might mean. I had to be brave and not flinch no matter what she did to me.

Dutch stood against the doorway, puffing on his pipe and wincing at every move of the tweezers. My father did not take his eyes off my bleeding face. He leaned forward, arms resting on his thighs. His face was five inches from mine. I could see him out of the corner of my eye. How long was it since I had seen my father's eyes dreamy and at peace? Was it ten months or ten years? I breathed deeply as Nurse Washington turned to set a sliver of glass in a metal tray.

I had ruined everything for Dutch. I had wrecked Christopher Crawford's trains, and that would get everyone into big trouble. Worst of all, I had no chance now of getting the reward from Mr. Pettishanks and buying an orange ranch for my hardworking dad.

What had been the key the night of the robbery that allowed me to shoot through time and space itself? Why could I not do it again? I could not answer because I could not remember.

Nurse Washington picked out all the glass at last and then went to work on my hands. My hands were scraped strawberry raw on the palms. Fake grass had embedded itself in the skin. She washed out the worst of it, put on antiseptic, and gauze-bandaged them. She taped my knee and put a dressing on the wound on my head.

Then she listened carefully with a stethoscope to my breathing and heart. She concentrated with her eyes closed and for quite some time pressed me in various places on my chest and back.

"Does this hurt?" she kept asking.

"A little," I answered. "I can't breathe as deeply as I'd like, but it's okay."

"You don't have pneumonia," she said. "You don't have pleurisy rales. There is no apparent internal bleeding." She tapped her stethoscope against her chin. "Other than this fall, has he . . . has he been in any serious accident?" she asked my dad. "Within the last two weeks?"

"No," Dad said.

"Any kind of shock recently?"

"No," said Dad.

I did not want to tell her about being shot out of a cannon and landing on a Lionel layout from a bank lobby in Cairo, Illinois, a few days ago, not to mention the same thing happening all over again as the taxicab backed away from the curb outside the station in L.A.

"Funny," she said. "I was a war nurse in 1918. Believe me, I saw everything there was to see. This young man has definitely suffered some sort of recent trauma. There's puffiness in the chest and small breaks of capillaries all over the trunk. The internal organs have been given a ramming of what we call g-forces. High-speed shock. I've seen it in pilots whose planes threw them around at great velocity. I've seen it in shell shock. Usually there are terrible injuries, for instance in a car accident. This is most peculiar. I can't put my finger on it, but I have seen this condition in wartime. And yet . . ."

"Are you sure?" asked my dad.

"As sure as God made little green apples," she answered.

Nurse Washington ended my treatment with a hefty injection. "It's just a little sulfa drug and a smidge of morphine for the pain," she said. "It's the latest and the greatest, and it will prevent infection."

I nearly passed out at the sight of the needle just as I did when Dr. Peasley back in Cairo gave me my annual tuberculosis and diphtheria shots. She quickly gave me smelling salts to bring me out of my daze.

My dad paid her five dollars cash from his worn-out, paper-filled wallet. Dutch made him take it back. "The whole thing's my fault," said Dutch, and he stayed my father's hand, dropping his own five spot on the nurse's desk. "I made him do it."

Somewhere outside an ambulance wailed. The siren light, red and rotating, cast its reflection through the window onto Nurse Washington's spotless white uniform. The doors of the Mercy Hospital flew open with her next emergency.

"So sorry," I said, sitting up and wiping my nose. "I'm scared of needles!"

"You're going to have trouble in the army, Oscar," Nurse Washington said sadly.

I lay crumpled in the cushiony rear seat of Dutch's car as he drove us back to the Brown Derby and Dad's truck. Dutch eased through the night and the streets of the big city.

"Trouble is not the word for it," I heard Dutch say to Dad. "The army'll make short work of our boy." Dutch went quiet for a few moments. Then he spoke, dreamily: "Something has happened to Oscar," he said. "The psychoanalyzers would explain it by amnesia or some other fancy word. But something much stranger than that has happened to Oscar, because he *is* eleven years old! Look in his eyes. That's no man! He's still a boy or I'm a whirling dervish. Hell or high water, Pop, we'd better get him back to 1931 or he's a goner."

"But how?" asked my dad.

"Why didn't it work today?" asked Dutch almost to himself. "What went wrong? Was it the wrong train? The wrong atmosphere?"

I did not wake until Sunday morning when the telephone in Dad's apartment rang.

CHAPTER 10

"I collect perfect crimes!" said Mr. H. He
was a perfectly pear-shaped man, with a pear-shaped
head. His face was as pink as a baby's. He spoke in
a cut-glass English accent. I had only heard a fake
Englishman speak once, on "Our Gal Sunday," a
drama that Aunt Carmen never missed on the radio.

"Your father is an honorable chap," Mr. H. said,
pulling the tops of his knife-creased trousers ever so
neatly upward to sit without wrinkling them. "He
came all this way back to fix the layout. I suppose
Alma terrified him about Miss Crawford's temper.

We all shake in our shoes when we think of Miss Crawford and her famous temper."

Mr. H. also did not mention my bandages and crutch, which made me very grateful because I felt like a complete fool for diving into an electric train layout like someone from the loony bin. We sat alone in his study, he and I, while Dad was downstairs working on the layout. Dad had been able to assemble all the materials he needed to repair the layout from one of the movie studio's scenery departments. Thanks to Dutch, we got porch screening, plaster of paris, and enamel paint of the right colors on a Sunday, when the hardware stores were all closed.

Miss Chow appeared with pictures for Mr. H. to autograph, which he did in a looping swoop of the pen. She also brought him a cone-shaped glass filled with a brilliantly clear, gassy-looking drink. Mr. H. put one index finger into the drink and swirled the lemon rind around. Then he picked it out and nibbled the end of it. "Dutch told my wife, Alma, all about you and the bank robbers," he said. "It was a perfect crime!" He smiled. "I make mystery movies, I suppose you'd say," said Mr. H. "Suspense dramas."

"Yes, sir," I answered, sitting on the edge of my chair.

He went on, pulling a small notebook from his jacket and wetting the tip of his pencil with his tongue. "I recall the Christmas Eve Massacre well from the newspapers. First came the brutal murder of the guard, the stolen unmarked money, the apparent kidnapping of the boy, the reward—a handsome one, if I may say so. Then the manhunt with the bloodhounds. The aunt gave the police an article of the boy's clothing. The police let the dogs smell it and turned the dogs loose everywhere around Cairo. In the woods, down the dirt roads. Nothing. Nothing was ever found. Tell me something, Oscar," said Mr. H.

"Yes, sir?"

"Last night when I came home, Alma told me the story. I telephoned the head man at the FBI here in Los Angeles, Detective Hissbaum, an old friend. He remembers the crime well. He knew the detective who was in charge of the case back then. He provided me with a detail or two not written up in the newspapers. Do you mind if I ask you about it?"

"No, sir!"

Mr. H. sipped his drink and took another small nip of the lemon slice. "In the pocket of the missing boy's winter coat, the FBI found a paper. On it, in a boy's handwriting, was a two-hundred-eighty-eight-word poem. Can you tell me what that might have been?"

I frowned. "Of course," I said. "It was Kipling's poem 'If.' My aunt Carmen made me write it out ten times every night. That was my master copy. It was written in a code I used for memorizing."

I imagined which clothes the police had been given by Aunt Carmen. Did they give my worn socks or my pajamas to the police? Were my old corduroys slobbered over by a bunch of huge dogs?

"And can you recite that poem?" Mr. H. asked me.

"Easy!" I took a deep breath, "'If you can keep your head while all about you / Are losing theirs and blaming it on you . . .'"

When I finished, he said, "No one could fake that." He swallowed the rest of his drink. "My dear boy," he went on with a smile, "we are in Hollywood, not the Midwest, with all its glories. So you needn't call me sir. Mr. H. will do nicely."

"Yes, sir," I agreed.

"Please tell me everything you remember about the evening of December 24, 1931."

I launched into it, sitting deeply back in my chair, which was as comfortable as a bed and upholstered in a slick silvery leather.

I described catching the number 17 bus to the bank the night before Christmas. "It was snowing. I rang the bell on the side of the bank's front doors as I always did. Mr. Applegate, the night watchman, came up and unlocked the doors. I threw my coat on a chair. I think he said, 'Look at that darn snow! It's coming down like the blizzard of '88. We might never get home.' But right off, I spotted this heavy engine dangling over the beautiful blue glass river. I ran over to catch it so it wouldn't fall and shatter the glass."

"Did Mr. Applegate lock the bank after you came in?"

"No, sir. I usually did that, and I forgot, and I forgot to turn the alarm switch back on." I grimaced with the memory of my carelessness. "Dad and Dutch say it's not my fault the thieves got in and killed Mr. Applegate, but I know it was."

Mr. H. laughed explosively. "My dear boy," he

said, "these psychos would have shot out the door lock and turned off the alarm themselves in two seconds. They had the joint cased. You are certainly not at fault. It was their guns that killed Mr. Applegate."

"I'm not even a little bit at fault?" I asked Mr. H.

"Not one tenth of a percent out of a hundred," said Mr. H. "What happened next, Oscar?"

I finished my story. In my heart was a tiny window of lightness that had not been there a moment before. One little shard of memory jumped out of the blue and in front of me. I suddenly remembered one of the thugs' voices shouting a name.

I told Mr. H., and he wrote it down. "It was Mackey or McKey. Something like that. Someone pulled a gun on me. I heard the shot fired, but I had already jumped."

"Jumped?"

"Yes. With my eyes closed and holding my breath as if I were jumping into the wild blue yonder. I landed on the layout, but they couldn't see me because I was already as small as the make-believe tin people on the layout. I got on the next train and then changed in Chicago. When I woke up on the Golden State Limited, I felt all banged up, as if

I'd fallen out of a skyscraper window. But nothing was actually broken or bruised. That's when I met Dutch. He was in the bunk below me."

Three times Mr. H. walked me through the story. Each time I remembered a little more about the robbery, but the memory as a whole stood just to the side of my vision.

"Your story would make a good movie," said Mr. H. with an unhappy sigh, "but, alas, we don't have the special effects yet to make it believable. It would be like filming the *Titanic* using a ten-foot model in a studio tank. It would be a terrible movie."

He stood and picked up his glass. "I must go, Oscar. Alma and I are invited to a very boring cocktail party. I would rather listen to you. However, your father wishes to finish his work on the layout downstairs." He held out his hand to shake mine while bending and whispering in my ear. "I, alone," he said, "actually believe that you are still eleven years old, Oscar. And that you evidently managed to get onto a Lionel train."

"You believe me?" I asked.

"Of course! Look at your haircut. No man of twenty has a boy's haircut with a cowlick sticking up like a tent pole! Cowlicks calm down in late puberty."

"Dearest!" called Alma from upstairs. "We're late!" Mr. H. bolted up the stairs much more quickly than I thought a pear-shaped man could ever run.

Down in the Crawford basement, my dad was at work restoring Christopher Crawford's Hell Gate Bridge. "Gonna take hours to fix her, Oscar," Dad said. He handed me a pair of needle-nose pliers.

I examined the damage I'd caused jumping into the layout the night before. "I feel like a fool for wrecking everything, Dad," I said.

Dad grinned with a piece of copper wire in his mouth. He looked me up and down. I was bandaged up, with my knee taped and my hand in gauze. "Looks like you did more wreckage on yourself," he said. He had a full array of tools on the table. Little screwdrivers, special pliers, and glue. He picked up a small clamp and held one of the pylons in place while he glued it back together.

"This is like the old days, son," he muttered happily.

We worked side by side in the basement until the ruined layout began to take better shape. Dollops of plaster of paris had to dry over the screens in the precise East River banks where my foot had wrecked the original ones. Like a jeweler, I fit a score of tiny glass panes to restore Denver's Union Station. My big fingers got in my way.

Suddenly Dad winked at me. "Let that plaster dry, Oscar," he said. He pulled out a cigar and brought fifteen red-and-white Lionel boxes up from under the layout table. They were stamped PROTOTYPE and unopened. Out of the boxes came a silver train, twelve cars long.

"What is it?" I asked. I had only once seen such a wonderful train, and that was in a picture. It gleamed like sterling silver. On the nose of the streamlined engine was an enameled red eagle emblem.

"Remember, Oscar? It's the President," said my dad.

"Of course I remember!" I said. "That train was in the catalog that came in the mail the night you told me we had to sell the trains."

Dad puffed a few smoke rings of delight. "Lionel never actually sold many of these. Too expensive! But look at this, Oscar! The whole thing's made of pure polished nickel! And see! Every car has a different president on the seal. . . . Right here's the Coolidge, Harding, Wilson, Taft, TR, McKinley . . . it goes right through back to Lincoln."

I could see why the President was so expensive. It had a circling searchlight on its observation car. It worked, of course. Sure enough, on a plush seat, which changed into a bed at the push of a lever, sat the little tin girl with pigtails.

Dad opened the tiny door of the dining car. With an eyeglass screwdriver, he showed me the galley's cupboards. Two of the cabinets lay cunningly hidden beneath the seats of the diner's booths. The doors slid back and forth as if someone might just come along and fill them up with cans of soup and frozen steaks. "Keen little hidden closets!" Dad remarked. "No wonder this baby cost an arm and a leg."

"Even George Washington's got his name on the diner!" I said. "I wonder how he'd like that if he knew!"

"Let's let her rip!" said my dad. "It's probably the only one still in existence. I wonder where Mrs. Crawford ever got this prototype."

I nodded to the upstairs. "Dad, I bet movie stars are so rich they get everything they want overnight."

Dad put the train together, carefully joining the couplings. "We've got a better life, Oscar," he declared, very seriously. "So long as we keep ahold of it. You've got me, and I've got you, and from what I hear, that's a heck of a lot more than poor little adopted boy Christopher Crawford or his divorce-happy mama will ever have in this world!"

He tilted back in his seat and pulled the throttle. The President streaked over the tracks, through the tunnels like an arrow, faster and quieter than any other train we'd ever run. Dad switched the Golden Gate to a siding and sent the President from L.A. over the foothills of the Rockies, over the plains, and into Chicago on the regular L.A.–Chicago run.

"How about running her all the way to Grand Central?" said my dad, drawing fully on his cigar. He sidelined the Twentieth Century express train in Dearborn Station and sent the President flying past the Great Lakes loop over the heartland of America to New York City's Grand Central Terminal.

The late-day sun played in through the basement

windows of the Crawford mansion, casting deep, soft shadows on the layout's mountains. Upstairs in this house were famous people, their expensive furniture polish, and their oriental carpets. But down here things weren't too different from our basement in Cairo, where we had not a care in the world.

But we were not in Cairo, and the United States Army was coming to get me in less than twenty-four hours.

"Oscar," Dad said after a few coast-to-coast traversings of the President, "we're still in the soup. An eleven-year-old boy in the army's gonna spend most of his time throwing up in the brig."

"What's the brig, Dad?" I asked.

"It's the cooler, son. The slammer. It's where they put the recruits who won't march in a straight line."

"Are we going to Montana, Dad?" I asked.

He answered, "Oscar, as soon as the banks open after breakfast tomorrow, we're on our way. Got three hundred and fifty dollars saved up. We'll go to Montana." He waved in the general direction of the north. "We'll find a little cabin in the mountains someone's forgotten about. I'll get a job as a park ranger. You can catch fish, shoot game, and do the cooking, just like home. We'll get you all the schoolbooks you need to keep up. And we'll wait for you to grow up and really be twenty-one. Then we'll come back and no one will be the wiser. If the army still wants you when you're really twenty-one, then you'll serve your country like every other red-blooded American. Okay, Oscar?"

"Okay, Dad!" I said. *Fish,* I thought. I'd never cooked fish before. But we would be together, Dad and I, and that was not going to change if a team of wild horses tried pulling us apart.

Mr. H. sauntered downstairs in his dinner jacket and gazed in admiration at Dad's work.

"I won't be able to paint any more until morning," said Dad. "Plaster's got to dry."

"In that case, you are welcome to spend the night in the guest suite," said Mr. H.

Around eight o'clock, Dad and I took a break for sandwiches brought in by the lovely Miss Chow, who said not one word.

Dad and I worked until ten on the broken windows in the Denver station. Then we stumbled upstairs. "Oscar," said my dad, "I didn't tell Dutch or Mr. H. or anybody about this plan of mine. Just between you and me. Okay?"

"Yes, Dad."

"We'll go tomorrow morning, Oscar," he continued. "If we hurry, we'll make the 11:22 local for Seattle, then change to the 7:41 to Billings, Montana."

On the pillow of my bed were silk guest pajamas, neatly folded. I put them on. I had never worn silk in my life.

There was a modest tap on my door.

"Yes?" I said.

"Excuse me! Miss Chow here!"

"Yes, Miss Chow?" I opened the door.

"Toothbrush and soap," said Miss Chow. She had all the amenities neatly assembled on one of her silver trays. I took them and thanked her.

"And something else," said Miss Chow.

"Yes?" I asked.

She smiled. "Miss Chow hears everything! I will let you open your locked door of memory in the Oscar mind! Easily. Easily!" she said. "Chinese method going back two thousand years!"

CHAPTER 11

Miss Chow sat down right next to me on my bed. From a velvet-lined box she produced a black rock shaped roughly like a ball. It was glass and semi-see-through. Somewhere inside darted a little luminescent fish, or what seemed to be a fish. But it wasn't a fish. It couldn't be.

"What is this?" I asked Miss Chow.

"Translate to Star Stone," she answered. "Very rare. We find these in north China near Harbin. Sometimes the Star Stone appears in the river. Sometimes under the ginkgo tree. Very valuable. People pay a lot of money for Star Stone on the black market. Madame Chiang Kai-shek, first lady of China, has the Star Stone to help her husband fight the war against the Japanese. Miss Chow asks you just relax, please. Just look at little star inside stone. Just relax in that bed. Don't take your eye off little star. Okay?"

I did as she told me.

"That's it, Oscar. Now you rub the Star Stone. Heat from your body will make the star jump around. You concentrate on that star until Miss Chow comes back in the room, please."

Again I did as I was told. The heat of my hands and my stomach where the stone rested made the little internal star swim around like crazy in its round black home. Something warm as a summer night settled over and into me. All anxieties dwindled out of my mind. Nothing seemed to matter but the tiny moving light in my hands. My eyes darted in unison with it as I lay in a state of alert quiet. The bedroom door opened without a sound. Miss Chow tiptoed back in so silently I would not have known she was there but for the light in the hallway spilling through the door.

I heard a tiny chuckle in her whisper. "Your

father fast asleep under his blanket. He did not wait for Miss Chow's toothbrush and silk pajamas."

I smiled a response but kept my eyes on the stone.

"How you feel, Oscar?" she asked, again in a whisper.

"Ahhhhhh!" was all I could answer.

She took the stone from me and crossed my hands on my belly.

"Now you close the eyes. Look up inside the eyes without moving the head, okay? Okay? Roll the eyes back in the head. Good! Good! Good!" said Miss Chow softly. She waited a minute and listened to my breathing.

"Tell Miss Chow your name. Speak slowly, please."

"Oscar Ogilvie Junior."

"How old you, Oscar?"

"Eleven years old."

"Now you tell Miss Chow what happened inside that bank, please."

The stubborn troll in the corner of my mind's eye began to move to the center of my vision. I spoke without hesitation. "I am pressing my face to the fake grass on the bank's western slope layout. The church bells ring five times out in the street. Suddenly there is a funny noise. Two men are rushing in! They have stockings over their faces, which they rip off. One of them hits Mr. Applegate on the head. Snow flies off his shoulders. Mr. Applegate goes down. Oh, my God. Oh, my God!"

Miss Chow's hand immediately soothed mine. She asked, "He has a name, this man?"

"Yes, Stackpole!" I said immediately. The memory was clear as day. "This man is big. He's stooped over with long arms like a monkey. He grabs Mr. Applegate and blindfolds him with a stocking mask in half a second. Then both men look around the bank. The monkey man's all pitted with acne. He has one thick eyebrow going right across his face and a mustache like . . . it looks like a black caterpillar. The other man is a little runt. His hair is tufty and kind of reddish-yellow-colored. He has a broken nose and a big jagged scar on his forehead.

"At first they don't see me. They're too busy blindfolding and beating Mr. Applegate."

I began to actually use the voices of Stackpole

and McGee—I remembered his name clearly now. Their voices rang freshly in my mind, as if they were there in the bedroom at that moment.

"'Put your mitts up and throw the keys to the teller's drawer over to me! Right now, right now! Do it!' yells Stackpole. 'McGee, grab them keys and get the cash fast!'"

"Mr. Applegate empties his pocket of his keys before they bind his hands behind him. I duck and then stand as low and still as I can against the side of the layout.

"McGee grabs the keys and rushes over to the teller's window. I hear him yank open the drawer. He throws it on the tiles below. It crashes. He yells, 'There's no money! Where's the cash, you dumb sap?'

"Mr. Applegate is gasping for breath. 'Every night it gets put in the vault,' he explains. 'It's locked away! I don't have the keys. It's a combination lock, and there's an alarm. Just leave now, please! You can't get the money!' Mr. Applegate pleads with them. 'And I can't get it for you!' The words come out of him fast and terrified. I remain absolutely quiet like a boy of stone. All around the huge layout, the trains are circling and whistling as if nothing is happening.

"'Shoot the vault open, cheese-face!' McGee growls to his partner.

"Mr. Applegate is lying far out of reach from me across the room. I can't help him! I can't help him or they'll see me. I can hear my heart *bam-bam-bamming* away. *Go!* I pray. *Just take the money and go!*

"The two men shoot their way through a pair of iron gates and then shoot three times into the lock on the main vault.

"It takes them only a few seconds. They grab two carryalls of cash, then they come crashing out again. McGee gives the bank a last look over and then he sees me.

"'Who the hell is *that*?' he says.

"'It's a kid. Some stupid kid!' says Stackpole.

"'He seen us! He seen us! No witnesses, Stackpole,' yells McGee.

"'We can't shoot a kid. Let's snatch him. We'll let him go when we get to El Paso. Then we'll cross the border and let him find his way in the desert.'

"'I'm gonna rub him out now,' says McGee. 'We don't need no flat tires with us.'

"'We *can't* kill *a kid*,' Stackpole argues. 'This is already a box job! They'll have the whole FBI after us by morning. C'mon, we'll blindfold him and take him to Blue Island until things go quiet.'

"'That's kidnapping, you dumb mug!' says McGee. 'The kid is a goner. I'm gonna blow his little head off!'

"McGee raises his gun. He squints one eye along the sight, and Mr. Applegate yells, 'Jump, Oscar! Jump!' and McGee whips around and shoots Mr. Applegate. Once in the head, once in the heart. Blood everywhere. Oh, Mother of God!" I put my hands over my eyes and felt my whole body shake.

Gently Miss Chow touched my arm. "Then what, Oscar? Then what?" she asked.

"It's ridiculous," I answered. "I jump like I've never jumped in my life. McGee pulls the trigger on me. Bang! I hear him shoot me. But it's too late. He can't see me anymore because he doesn't know where to look. I'm in a seafoam juniper bush next to the Dune Park Station on the layout. And I'm small. I'm so small that when the train comes around the bend and stops, I just get right on it and sit right down and nobody thinks anything is strange at all."

I must have been anxious because Miss Chow

had a handkerchief out and was clearing my brow with it. "They shoot you?" she asked.

"McGee is five feet away. He aims the gun directly at my forehead. I see him pull the trigger."

"And you just jumped?" asked Miss Chow calmly, as if perhaps I had hopped over a skip rope.

"Yes. That part was actually easy. It was like being shot out of a cannon. I was terrified they'd see me. I heard them chasing around, looking for me everywhere. Everywhere in the bank but not on the layout. That's all. Then the bank just faded. I wanted to help Mr. Applegate, but there wasn't any Mr. Applegate. I could feel the wind off the lake. I was at a train station on the South Shore Line, and I got on the first train that came along."

Miss Chow put the Star Stone back into my hands. Its blue-green eye calmed me, and she let me sit with it for many minutes.

"You feel better now?" she asked at last.

"Yes."

"The story is a miracle," said Miss Chow.

"I don't expect you to believe it," I said.

"Star Stone cannot produce the lie," said Miss

Chow. She put her hand on the stone. "Now, Oscar, this is what Miss Chow thinks!"

"Yes?" I ask. "Am I dead or alive, Miss Chow?"

"You are alive, Oscar. By the skin of the teeth! Chinese people know there is a small space between life and death, okay? Oscar got in that space one second before that bullet hit you. Oscar jumped into a parallel universe."

"Alongside."

"Yes, exactly. Both worlds are real thing. But this 1941 is not your world yet. You are still eleven-year-old boy in your big man's body. You need to go home."

"Home?"

"So, Oscar, you cannot get on the train again unless you are very, very scared. You understand? That is why yesterday you banged up the Oscar head and the Oscar knee, because you tried without being scared. The word *jump* is the secret key!" She tapped one long fingernail on my knuckle. "You hear Miss Chow?"

"Yes," I whispered. "Yes."

"You not guilty of the night watchman's death.

You not guilty! So you will remember *everything* now!" she repeated.

Miss Chow slipped the Star Stone into its sack. On red silk slippers she left my room as silently as she had come.

CHAPTER 12

Mr. H. woke me when the sky outside my window showed its first streaks of morning light. "I understand that Miss Chow and her mysterious stone worked wonders on you, Oscar," he said. He handed me a glass of fresh orange juice.

"I remember everything now," I answered. Miss Chow and her Star Stone were clearly part of Mr. H.'s plan. What was next?

"Good," said Mr. H. "Now, Oscar. Last night at the cocktail party, Dutch and I had a word with

Detective Hissbaum. You remember he happens to be the head of the Federal Bureau of Investigation here in L.A. I chatted him up. You understand, Oscar, ten years ago you were a material witness to a felony and your account of it must be reported to the police. Otherwise we are concealing evidence to a crime."

In my bed, I nodded and pulled the blanket up to my chin.

"And so," Mr. H. concluded, "Detective Hissbaum is going to pay us a visit. Hizzy's a good egg. A diamond in the rough, but a good egg nonetheless. He's coming here for breakfast."

Dutch was not going to miss a minute of breakfast with the head of the FBI West. He showed up carrying with him a square tin of Vermont maple syrup.

Alma cooked us all French toast. Miss Chow winked at me and fanned out the morning newspapers on the dining-room table. There was the *Los Angeles Times,* the *Press-Telegram,* the *Van Nuys News,* and the *Star-News.* My fifth-grade class photograph was plastered all over the front pages of four newspapers.

"Who leaked this to the papers?" asked Mr. H. icily. I couldn't have imagined Mr. H.'s pleasant voice with such cold, hard anger in it. "I don't want anyone to know Oscar is here." he said. "Publicity brings trouble!"

When Detective "Hizzy" Hissbaum arrived, he had a fairground voice and face to go with it. "It seems a reporter overheard our conversation at the party last night, chum," explained Detective Hissbaum to Mr. H. Pal, if the boy's the genuine article," he continued, "the story'll be headlined in every paper in the country tomorrow morning."

Hissbaum never took his hawk gaze off me. In his

hand was a stack of old snapshots of me, my fourth- and fifth-grade pictures, which had been enlarged to big glossies. One had me grinning in my choir-boy robes. Detective Hissbaum shot glances from the photos to me and back again, eating his French toast without even looking down at his plate. "Kid," he said when he'd finished his coffee, "December 1931, there was a forty-eight-state alert out for you. All these pictures have been in our files ever since the Christmas Eve Massacre. Head of Chicago FBI was a top man. Best in the business. Name of Pearly Gates. It was a prime case, Pearly's baby. He never cracked it. We had ten teams of bloodhounds look-ing for you, Oscar, a hundred agents. Where the devil have you been?"

Squirming, I looked at Dutch and my dad for help.

"I've heard everything there is to hear, kid," Mr. Hissbaum assured me. "You can't surprise me. What'd they do? Keep you in a cage full of mon-keys? Put you in a closet? Tie you to a tree?"

Fresh with the details from the night before, I began.

Detective Hissbaum popped a cigar from his shirt pocket when I finished. It was a Macanudo. He lit it up. "I'm going to test you, Oscar," he said, blowing out a blue lungful of smoke. "Take your time, boy, but get the right answer. You got one chance with me. Okay?"

"Yes, sir!" I answered.

"How many shots did the thieves use to crack the door to the vault?" he asked.

I thought and pictured it. "Three," I answered.

"How many shots killed the guard?"

"One in the heart. One in the head."

Detective Hissbaum nodded. "Close your eyes, boy. Think hard. One of 'em dropped something during the robbery. What was that thing that he dropped, and what was in it?"

I went over the entire crime again in my mind. Dropped? What dropped? I started at the beginning. Yes, of course! "The head teller's cash drawer," I answered. "And nothing was in it."

Detective Hissbaum expelled a mouthful of smoke and glared at me. "You're the real McCoy, kid. No one else in the world could possibly know these details." A big inhale and exhale of cigar smoke. "But son of a gun, we're ten years too late! If those goons were headed El Paso way, they'd have flipped across the border into Mexico in no time." Hissbaum used an awful word to describe the two. Alma drew in breath, and Hissbaum said, "Excuse my French. Sorry, Mrs. H., I got carried away. But I know who these crumbs are. Mickey 'Hands-off' Stackpole was a two-bit punk on parole for battery in a diner robbery. Buck 'Gaspipe' McGee did ten years in Folsom for sticking up a jewelry store in Kansas City. Christmas Day, 1931, they went into the unknown without a trace. Both of 'em. No doubt about it, they're living the life of Riley someplace warm. Paraguay, maybe. They could be anywhere. Siam! Persia! French West Africa!"

Dutch put in, "They'd have the money to alter their appearances with plastic surgery!"

"You were on ice for ten years, kid!" said Detective Hissbaum. "Where?"

"I was . . . on my way out here," I answered shakily.

"Whadja do? Walk on your hands?"

"I was on a train."

"What kind of train?"

I shook my head and looked to Dutch, who was, for once, tongue-tied.

"Look, kid," said the detective, "I got two of my best agents coming up here in a squad car as we speak. So far your story checks out. But we can't find these crumbs unless you tell us where ya been for the last ten years. Where did they keep you? Did they beat you up? Threaten you?"

At that moment there was a sharp rap on the door.

"My guys!" said Detective Hissbaum. Dutch left the room and strode down the hall to open the front door. But instead of two detectives, there were two soldiers in khaki uniforms and puttees standing on the doorstep. With no invitation whatever, they stepped past him into the hallway. They spotted me immediately, sitting at the dining-room table one room down.

The officer was a ruddy-faced lieutenant with curly black hair. He held a copy of the *Los Angeles Times* to his chest. Under my eleven-year-old photo was the screaming headline:

KIDNAPPED OGILVIE BOY FOUND IN HOLLYWOOD!

The officer grinned broadly. He saluted Detective Hissbaum smartly and strutted into the dining room. Following him marched a beefy corporal with a pair of handcuffs at the ready.

"You're under military arrest, Ogilvie," snapped the officer. "I'm the deputy draft officer for Los Angeles County. The minute I saw the morning paper with your face all over the front page, I called your draft board officer back in Cairo, Illinois. Seems you didn't register for the U.S. Army!"

"But—" I began.

"Hold your horses, Lieutenant!" my dad broke in. He stood up and tried to look reasonable and not-to-be-fooled-with all at once. Dad would be no match for this burly draft officer—I knew that much.

"Don't interfere with the army, sir!" snapped the lieutenant, and he turned to me again. "You'll cool your heels in an army brig for a month for draft evasion, Private. Then I'll recommend you for the combat parachute troops in Siberia. You get to jump right out of a plane and help the Russkies fight the Krauts in the Arctic Circle!" The officer smirked. "You may not remember me, but I sure remember you. You're fresh meat, Private Ogilvie!"

I had never made the acquaintance of an army officer in my short life. How could this lieutenant possibly know me?

"You're wrong!" I pleaded. "I'm only eleven years

old. I'm in the fifth grade. You can't draft me!" my voice cracked.

Dad stepped around the table. Dutch got to his feet and said, "You're on private property, Lieutenant. You need a search warrant to come in here!"

Detective Hissbaum shook his head sadly. "It's the long arm of Uncle Sam, Dutch. No warrants, no questions, no civil laws apply to the army."

"That's right, sir!" the soldier said smartly.

The voice. Suddenly I knew that voice!

The lieutenant lowered the paper and tossed the *Los Angeles Times* onto the table. Sure enough, on his uniform breast pocket was his name in gold stitching, LT. CYRIL PETTISHANKS.

As it happened, Miss Chow began to clear the breakfast table just as the corporal lunged forward at me with his handcuffs open like crab claws. For a single awkward moment, she stepped in the corporal's way, her silver tray stacked full of syrupy, buttery plates. "Excuse me!" she said, smiling as the corporal stumbled into the stack of plates, allowing precious seconds for me to get to my feet and slip away.

"Oscar," she said under her breath, "go downstairs

through the kitchen! Get on the train! Get on the same train you came here on, the Golden State, Oscar!"

There was no time for the elevator. I raced into the kitchen and down the back stairway, ignoring my gauze-bound hands and taped, swollen knee. Cyril charged after me, one flight of stairs behind. I had felt sorry for Cyril. How had he turned from a Saint Bernard into a pit bull terrier? How would I escape and get to Montana with my dad?

I dived into the train room and threw all the switches on the wall. The trains roared to life. The signals blinked, the gates went up and down, and the whistles blew like the howling prairie wind.

"You little worm!" shouted Cyril. "If it wasn't for you, my old man wouldn't have shunted me off to military school for seven godforsaken years. . . . No girls, up at five in the morning, food worse than the dog pound! You're going to pay for that, you little poetry-spouting twerp!"

From the kitchen stairwell I heard Miss Chow. She gave a happy yell, as if she were calling a baby to her arms. "Jump, Oscar!" she called. "Jump!"

And, of course, I was scared spitless of Cyril and his handcuff-wielding sidekick. I grabbed my duffle bag of little boys' clothes, which had fallen on the floor, and I jumped. Like an Olympic high diver, I jumped!

CHAPTER 13

I landed on the yellow-brick pavement that ringed the station just beyond the taxi rank with its available top-lit cabs. Feverishly I prayed again, to every single one of the saints, that Cyril would not look at the Crawford layout too closely.

"Fade!" I wanted to yell to Cyril and the room and everything in the year 1941. "Fade away!" It did not fade fast enough. I looked up and tried to see Cyril's face. Had he noticed me? Was I just another one of the little tin toy people from up there? I heard kicking and banging under the table. He was looking for me underneath the layout. I took a chance and dashed up the station steps and into the station lobby. Leather easy chairs sprawled on the tiles. I ran past a hot-dog vendor and a newsstand, but I didn't have time to look at the newspapers. A loudspeaker blared, "All aboard for Chicago on the Golden State Limited, 9:17, departing in one minute from platform two. All aboard!"

My knee brace fell away, and I ran like a greyhound down the arched, tiled passageways to the platform. If I made it onto the train, Cyril would soon fade, and I would pull out of Los Angeles, homeward bound.

The Golden State Limited waited, steaming and purring its engine on platform two. I ran for the steps of one of its Pullman sleeper cars. Then something made me stop. It was the shadow of an enormous hand. I shrank behind a signal box that stood on the platform and watched as a brown khaki cuff, neatly bound with gold braid stripes, hovered over the tracks. Glinting on the third finger was a Missouri Military Prep class ring. The fingers twitched as if they were about to select and tweak up a piece of candy. Then the hand came down toward the engine of the Golden State.

Clear as a bell in my mind's ear rang the voice of Mr. Applegate: *"Cyril!"* he trumpeted. *"Cyril isn't even allowed near the trains. He likes to have accidents! The old man won't let him in the room with the layout!"*

I knew, of course, that Lieutenant Cyril Pettishanks, U.S. Army Recruiting Office, had heard Miss Chow yell Jump! as clearly as I had. The Crawford basement had no other exit but the stairway and elevator. There wasn't a nook or cranny in the room to hide in. I peered out an inch from my hiding place. Sure enough, I saw Cyril's huge face above me. He blinked a couple of times and then fastened on the layout in front of him. I could see every fiber in the weave of his army shirt, every pore and whisker on his jaw, magnified. In proportion, Cyril was so big, I could have fit into his front pocket.

I slithered back behind a hot-dog stand and held my breath. The big hairy hand from the big sleeve reached out for my train. Cyril lifted the engine of the Golden State, then he yanked the entire ten-car train from its track — Pullmans, tender, and caboose. Cyril shook each car like a jar full of candy, as if he thought I was in one of them. Each time, he cursed in disgust while I watched, hardly breathing, hiding

in the hot-dog stand. Cyril slammed each car of the Golden State down on the cement floor of the basement. The train and its engine, dining car, and sleepers broke into twisted pieces at his feet. "Get out of that damn train, Ogilvie!" Cyril yelled as he smashed each car. Through the intensifying fog of the fading room, I could just make out the voice of Corporal Handcuffs. He must have plodded down the stairs after Cyril. I could not see him, but I heard his voice whining loud and clear. "Jeez Louise, Lieutenant! You crazy? The boy ain't on no electric train. He's ex-caped onto the elevator. Let's go!"

Cyril swore, but he turned around to his corporal. With a squeal of brakes, another train had rounded the bend and pulled up into the slot where the Golden State had been. It did not stop. Whatever it was, wherever it was headed, I didn't care. I aimed for the moving steps and leaped into the safe depths of the interior.

"Go away!" I said between my teeth to the outside world of 1941. I didn't care if the train were heading for Timbuktu. I found a bunk in one of the smartly made sleeper cars just as the train left the station.

I didn't dare move for the longest time. When

I finally looked out of my bunk window, the landscape that whizzed by could have been anywhere. What train was I on? Union Pacific? Where was it going? Texas? Louisiana?

No breezy college man slammed into the compartment in the middle of the night and started singing "Rambling Wreck from Georgia Tech." As the hours passed, I missed Dutch more. I wished he were there to have steak and ice cream with. And I missed my dad. Would he know I'd made it this time? Would he cheer and know that I would try to get him back to Cairo and he'd be young again?

The train whistled its high shriek over what seemed to be desert, and we began our slow ascent into the mountains. *East!* I told myself. *At least we're going east.*

The train was unusually quiet. No conductor had called out the next stop or the dining car seatings. What railroad company ran this line? Atchison-Topeka? Canadian Pacific? My head ached and throbbed so much that I could only close my eyes and sleep.

In my dreams Miss Joan Crawford appeared, raven hair bobbing in rage, lips open in a full shout, grabbing Lieutenant Cyril Pettishanks by the collar of his shirt and smashing one of her cut-glass decanters over his head for messing up her son's trains.

In the middle of the night, I awoke, feeling grimy. I reached for the toiletry kit provided by the railway, and that's when I saw it. On the kit bag was the seal of the president. I was on the prototype! I wanted to cry out for my dad, but of course he was hundreds of miles away by this time.

Brushing my teeth, I suddenly looked in the mirror. I stared at my skinny, undeveloped ribs. My arms were twiggy. My cheeks were smooth, and there were no scars from glass on my face. My chest was purple as a bruised plum, but I didn't care. I was eleven again.

I opened my zip bag and pulled on my new Bullock's boys' shop clothes. In them I fell back on the bunk and slept the sleep of an Egyptian mummy.

I didn't wake until the late morning. The train was as quiet as a church. It raced over silent trackbeds in an uninteresting landscape of winter desert. Since I was hungry, I made my way to the dining car, but the car was empty. No crisp white linen or silver had been laid on its tables. No waiter smiled and snapped my napkin onto my lap for me. Outside the windows, a red-rock landscape peeled away at enormous speed. Stations rushed by so fast I could not read the nameplates that hung over their platforms.

Suddenly I saw her. She was about my age, about eleven. She sat primly on a blue plush seat, pigtails framing her face.

"Hello!" she said.

I did not have time to say another word. We were not alone. The train's conductor suddenly swayed in the door of the dining car, giving us the once-over.

"How did you get on this train, girlie?" the conductor asked in a none-too-friendly voice. "And you, punk? Howja get on this train?"

"None of your business!" replied the girl in pigtails. "I'm on it and that's that."

"What train is this, sir?" I asked.

The conductor growled, "It's a prototype on a test loop. Not in service yet. She don't take no passengers, she don't make no stops, and she don't serve no meals."

"Where is it going?" I asked. I already knew. I tried to remember if my dad had made a permanent track switch for the President to run nonstop to New York. Or would we stop in Chicago? I couldn't remember exactly what Dad had done the night before with the Crawford layout's tracks.

"This here train was sealed," the conductor grunted. "Ain't nobody allowed on or off. How'd you get on, kids? Say, wait a minute. Don't move!"

The conductor's voice shifted suddenly as if he might be sweet-talking a cornered dog. Keeping his eyes on us, he backed all the way down the aisle until he came to the door that connected with the next car. I did not have to be told that he was going to fetch someone, a security officer, someone to confine or arrest us. I remembered that the George Washington diner was the last car of the train. The President was rushing through what looked like New Mexico at more than eighty miles an hour. There was no escape. What would they do to this girl in the pigtails? Or to me?

I waited until the conductor had been out of the car a few seconds. "Get down!" I said. She hit the floor immediately. "Who are you?" she asked.

"Never mind that now. He's coming back!" I said.

"If they find me, I'm finished," said the girl. "I'll be in so much trouble it won't be funny!"

I grabbed her hand. It was cold and trembling. "See that locker under the booth? Right where your feet go? Slide the door with that push-button release! Get in there! Quick," I whispered. "He may not be familiar with this train yet."

The hidden locker was exactly the one my dad had shown me with his optometrist's screwdriver. It was a supply closet for the diner car's galley, but there was no chef and no kitchen prep and so it was quite empty. So was its mate, an opposite floor-level locker on the other side of the dining booth. I climbed into that one.

The girl slid open a vent to whisper through. "If they find me, they'll stop the train and take us off into the middle of nowhere. They'll hold me in some jail in the back of beyond and call my parents. Who knows?" she half shouted and half whispered over the sound of the train's wheels.

I closed the door over myself and held my breath as the footsteps returned. Three sets of feet, I guessed. There was no comment at first, only the slap of shoe leather back and forth on the floor of the dining car and the slamming of various doors and cabinets.

Finally one man's deep baritone muttered unintelligible words. Then it declared, "Harry, you're seeing things. Maybe it's time to retire."

"I swear to God and everything that's holy, Captain, there was two of them. I seed 'em clear as day, a shifty-looking little squirt and that girl sitting at the table large as life. Pigtails and Mary Jane shoes!" the conductor answered.

"They ain't here, Harry. No one ain't here! No one couldn't have got on the train nohow anyhow. Them doors was sealed until the last minute."

"It's a delusion," said another voice. "You been up too late, Harry. How many corn dogs you eat last night?"

"It ain't the corn dogs," Harry complained. But the argument died out and I could hear them retreating as Harry announced his intention to check every bunk and every compartment in the blasted train.

We lay hidden for what seemed like an eternity. After a while the thought occurred to me that Harry would be back alone, and this time he might do a more careful excavation of the dining car's cupboards. I squirmed out of my locker and tapped on the locker door opposite.

My voice was urgent. "Harry will come back here to the galley," I said. "After he's checked the other compartments. The others think he's been into the giggle water, but believe me he'll come back here and root through these cars like a hound dog. I'm going to the Abraham Lincoln, Pullman four. There's a tiny storage locker room behind the lavatory. We can wait there until he passes on to the next compartment."

There was a hesitation from the other side. Finally the girl asked, "How *did* you get on this train, and how do you know so much about it?"

CHAPTER 14

"Come on out," I said when finally I was convinced Harry would not return. "I'll show you where the sleeper car is." I still had managed not to answer her question.

The girl's name was Claire Bister. She had told me she was ten and a half years old and lived at the corner of Park Avenue and Seventieth Street, New York City. She had two light-brown pigtails with blue ribbon bows at the ends. Claire was skinny like me, with intelligent green eyes and a determined look on her face.

"What's your name?" she asked.

"Oscar Ogilvie," I answered. "I'm eleven years old and I come from Cairo, Illinois."

"You saved my life, Oscar Ogilvie," she said. "If we'd have been caught, they would have stopped the train and called my father, and Daddy would have called the police and would have been so mad it wouldn't even be funny. If there is anything I can ever do to repay you, I will!"

Right off the bat, Claire confided that she had run away from home.

"What did they do to you?" I asked.

"It got to be too much," said Claire. "They enrolled me in ballroom dancing lessons. I hate ballroom dancing. They bought me dolls and frilly dresses, and Mummy keeps talking about someday when I have a coming-out party. I don't ever want a coming-out party, and I refuse to have one!"

"What is that?" I asked. "Coming out of where?"

Claire sized me up and down for a couple of seconds.

"It's a stupid society thing," she said. "It's for girls at eighteen to dress in long white dresses with kid gloves and meet all the right boys and none of the wrong boys. That way all the rich boys marry rich girls and have rich babies and it just goes forward in a big horrible line. I won't do it. I won't go to boarding school, either. I just couldn't stand it anymore."

"Boarding school." I stumbled on the words a little. "Is that like a military academy?"

"Almost as bad," said Claire. "They make you wear an ugly old plaid uniform and force you to go to study halls and field hockey every waking minute of the day. I like to play baseball and football too. They won't let me."

"Why?" I asked. "Why do your folks want to send you away?"

"Mummy and Daddy have no time," answered Claire, "because of their parties and dinners and business and all that. Daddy's a busy lawyer. Mummy's a social butterfly. They think I'd be happier at Miss Pryor's Girls' Academy in the sticks of New Jersey. Fat chance!"

"I guess they'd think I was one of the wrong boys," I said.

"That's what I like about you, Oscar," Claire

answered, and she fixed me with a dead-certain look.

I hung on to the railing of her bunk. Claire's world might as well be life on the moon or in Hollywood to a poor boy from Cairo like me.

"How did you get on this train, Claire?" I asked after a minute of silence.

"You won't believe me," said Claire.

"I will believe anything," I said. "I mean I'm on it, too! You won't believe me either. No one does."

Claire blew out a mouthful of what-do-I-care air. "It was at Christmas," explained Claire. She kicked the blanket that lay folded at her feet. "It all started on Christmas vacation. During Christmas holidays, my parents always feel guilty. So they took me and my brother to FAO Schwarz."

"What's that?" I asked.

"It's a big, big toy store on Fifth Avenue. Biggest in the world. Six floors of toys. I wanted a train set just like my brother Maxwell's. Well, Daddy and Mummy said no. No, no, no. Trains are for boys, not for girls. So I couldn't have it. I had to have a doll. I told them I hated dolls, especially dolls in mink-trimmed coats. I threatened to toss any doll they gave me out my window into the middle of Park Avenue.

"Christmas morning I went downstairs early, way before anyone else was up. Sure enough, under the tree, there's Maxwell's train. A beauty. Daddy knows Mr. Cowen, who owns Lionel. Maxwell gets all the prototypes years before they get into the stores. So there's Maxwell's train, all silver and rocketlike. And there's my fancy lace and satin doll. Yick!"

"So what happened next?" I asked.

"I began to cry," said Claire. "I knew no matter what I ever said, they would never hear me, Claire. They would just hear a pretend Claire who liked dolls and was going to grow up and get married to the son of one of Daddy's friends at the club. So I lay down on the carpet under the Christmas tree and pushed the switch to start up Max's new train. It ran beautifully, quieter than his other trains. I began to picture myself with no dolls and no ballroom dancing. I pictured myself on the train, actually getting on the train.

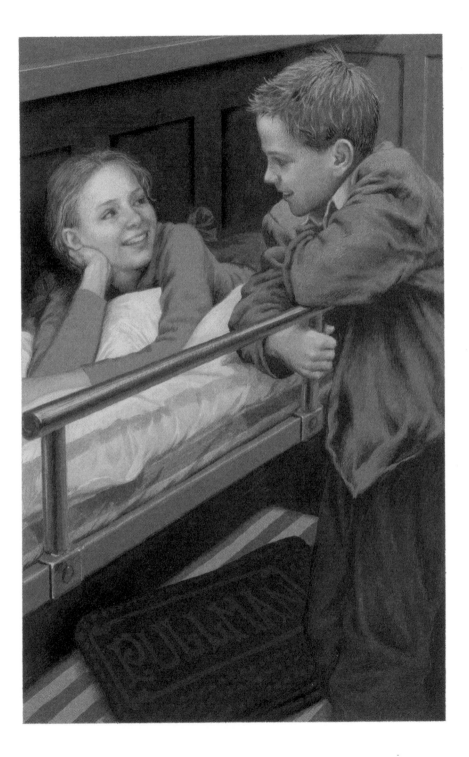

"Then Mummy came downstairs and she said, 'Claire, dear, that's your brother's train. Look at your beautiful doll, darling!'

"And so, I just . . . I just jumped on the train, and now I'm here."

"Were you scared?" I asked. "Is that how you jumped on?"

Claire frowned for a moment. "No," she said. "There's nothing to be afraid of in my apartment. Mummy and Daddy certainly aren't scary, and my brother is just a chucklehead. It was . . . it was longing. Just longing that made it happen, Oscar."

"I sure know about that," I said. "I spent a whole three months longing when my dad left home for California."

"Do you believe me, Oscar?" Abruptly Claire rolled her head toward me on her pillow and looked directly into my eyes.

I didn't blink. Why shouldn't I believe her? Claire's story was a lot easier to swallow than mine. "Yes," I answered. "It seems perfectly logical."

"Your turn to tell, Oscar," said Claire.

I began with the layout in the basement of our

house on Lucifer Street. I got to the Wall Street crash before Claire said a word. "That old crash is what started all our problems," I told her. "Right in the paper it said millionaires who lost all their dough in one day started jumping out skyscraper windows. The ones who didn't jump out windows wound up selling apples on the street for a nickel an apple."

Claire frowned. "Everyone lost their money?" she asked. "Everyone?"

"Not everyone," I said. "Mr. Pettishanks and all the people at the River Heights Country Club still got by, but the poor farmers couldn't buy any more tractors. John Deere laid off all its salesmen. My dad lost his job. Ordinary people like us, we went broke. We had to sell our house back to the bank; even our trains were sold to Mr. Pettishanks's bank."

"When was this crash?" asked Claire.

"October 29, 1929," I answered.

Claire frowned at this. "We haven't gotten to 1929, yet, Oscar. I left New York on December 25, 1926."

"You did?"

"Yes, and the train hasn't made a single stop longer than that little pause where you hopped on in Los Angeles. We went all the way west, and now we're going east again, and I'm starving. . . . I've had nothing but Wheaties and Carnation milk since I've been on the train. I found them in the galley."

I rooted in the pocket of my Bullock's boys' shop duffle and extracted the Hershey bar that Dutch had bought me before he left the L.A. station a week ago. Was it? Or was it ten years ago? Or had it not happened yet? But here was the Hershey bar, solid squares of chocolate with almonds. Claire ate it in four bites.

"I'm getting out at Chicago," I said. "The President train stops there. I'm sure of it. My dad put it on the Crawford layout tracks last night. He ran it through Christopher Crawford's Dearborn Station. The signal turned red, and the train stopped for a few minutes there."

"What?"

I sighed. I knew she wouldn't believe me. "Claire, when I got on this train, it was 1941. When I left Cairo for Los Angeles, it was 1931. I was in a time pocket. I traveled west for two thousand miles and got out in California. I gained ten years' time."

"Impossible!" said Claire.

"I think I'd better tell you about negative velocity and Professor Einstein's theory of relativity and time." I hesitated. "Time is like a river and—"

"Professor who?" asked Claire.

"It's higher math—"

"I can't even do lower math," Claire interrupted. "Let's skip that. Tell me about this crash instead."

The crash. I was shaky on the crash. I hadn't paid much attention to the newspapers. "You know where Wall Street is, Claire?"

"Yes, of course! My father works on Wall Street! He's a lawyer for a Wall Street bank."

"Well, Wall Street is where the crash happened. It was all over the *Cairo Herald*. Your dad better watch out in three years' time is all I can say!" I told her.

Dreamily, Claire traced a design in the windowpane fog beside her bunk. What was she thinking?

"Do you want me to go on with how I got on the train?" I asked her.

"Of course, Oscar. What happened next?"

As my words and memories spun out, I touched on Aunt Carmen's kidney-bean casseroles, on Mr.

Applegate saving my neck, on how he left the soaking wet *Fireside Book of Poetry* on the kitchen table and how it had been spotted by Willa Sue. I described Cyril and his hopeless rendition of the poem "If." Claire stopped me right there.

"That's my favorite poem!" she said. "Can you recite it?"

"Can I recite it!" I answered. "I could recite every blessed word of that thing with a bucket over my head and one foot in an anthill:

"If you can keep your head when all about you
Are losing theirs and blaming it on you . . ."

I finished it, as always, not missing a single word. Then Claire recited it with more gusto than I had. Then we said the whole of "If" together in unison, complete with the gestures and dramatic flourishes that Mr. Kipling himself no doubt used when he wrote the poem in 1891.

Our train raced through small towns somewhere in one of the square states. Street lamps winked by us in half seconds. The taillights of a truck vanished over the horizon on an empty road, and a firehouse whistle blew somewhere on a deserted street. I could just hear it through the heavy windows. Our train thundered past sidings, junctions, and the checkered gates of crossings, red flares flashing at our passing. Small stationmasters' houses whizzed by, all built alike of red brick by the railroad companies along the tracks. Outside each one, green glass signals of the all-clear lanterns swung on iron hooks and glowed like cat's-eyes in the coming evening. To the southwest, the sky darkened, a purplish black curtain sinking over the fiery leavings of the day's sun.

"Can you read the station names?" I asked Claire as they flickered past us in the darkness, the sleepy towns of the west.

"I can't. The train's going too fast to read them," said Claire, "but go back to your story, Oscar. What happened next?"

I got to the part about Stackpole and McGee slipping into the bank on Christmas Eve, whacking Mr. Applegate on the head, and pulling the gun directly on me. The memory was still fresh, and my voice was a little shaky in the telling of it.

"You jumped?" asked Claire.

"I had no choice. It was jump or die."

Claire listened to the rest of my story, through Dutch and Mr. H., Miss Chow and the breakfast appearance of Cyril Pettishanks in his army recruiter's uniform.

"And you did it again?" said Claire. "You got on another train? This one that we're on now?"

"Miss Chow yelled 'Jump!'" I said. "It was jump then or jump out of an airplane over Siberia to help the Russkies fight the Krauts."

"Who are the Russkies and who are the Krauts?"

My head was beginning to ache from Claire's questions. "I don't know why it's important," I said. "The war won't even start until 1941."

Claire went back to her window tracing. "You know something, Oscar?" she said. "Daddy would give his eyeteeth to know what's going to happen in the future, and so would all his friends. The future is his business. That's what the stock market is. Every morning over his oatmeal, Daddy says anyone who can read tomorrow's tea leaves gets rich."

"I thought your father was already rich," I said.

Claire snorted. "Oh, he's rich, all right. But you

have to understand about really wealthy people, Oscar. Most of 'em just try to double their money, then triple it. That's how they spend their days. Daddy'd give his right arm to know what you know, Oscar."

"Well," I said, "you can tell him someday, Claire."

"He would laugh," said Claire. "He'd never believe a single word. If he ever forgives me for running away from home, that is. They've probably got a thirteen-state alarm out for me. When I go home, they'll keep me in the apartment for a month. Then it'll be dolls and dancing lessons and white cotton gloves all over again."

Somewhere around a bend in the tracks, another train whistled. Where was it heading? Where might we be in the universe? The prairie states encircled us, farmhouses all asleep in the embrace of the night.

Together we clicked out our tiny bunk lamps. In the rolling darkness, I told Claire everything in my life, even the most private feelings that ever seemed important. She told me the same from the bunk underneath. We talked until neither of us could form words with our sleepy tongues.

Before dawn, the sound changed and the train slowed. I woke. I could read the station names now. Naperville sailed by. I knew Naperville lay just to the west of Chicago. I woke Claire, tapping on the metal bedpost that ran up the side of the bunks. "We're coming into Chicago!" I whispered. "We're slowing down! I'm going to make a run for it!"

"Oh, Oscar!" said Claire. "I'll never see you again!"

"I have to go, Claire!" I said, bumping out of my bed. "But I'll find a way!"

We waited together at the door of the train. "Good-bye!" I said as the Dearborn Station platform appeared by our side.

Suddenly the train jerked away from it and veered left onto another track. Then it sped up, and my heart sank. We hadn't stopped at all. We raced on by Dearborn Station; the Twentieth Century waited on a layby on our left side. We were heading south of the Great Lakes and east to New York.

I sat on my bunk and watched suburban Chicago pass without interest. "Oh, no, no, no!" I moaned.

"I'll never see my dad again. I want to go home and now I can't!"

"I did something terrible, Oscar," whispered Claire.

"What did you do?" I asked, without much interest.

"Last night after we stopped talking, I said my prayers. And I wished as hard as I could that you would somehow stay on the train. I promised to be good for the rest of my life. And that's what happened. God heard me," said Claire. "And now I have to make it up to you."

"No, Claire," I replied. "I'm afraid it's my dad's doing."

"Your dad?"

I sighed heavily at the prospect of explaining again. "Two nights ago," I said, "Dad and I were running the trains on the Crawford layout. Dad messed around with the track configuration. Dad wanted to send this President prototype across the whole country on a direct run. He must have side-lined the regular Chicago–New York trains, put a Y joint in the tracks at Chicago, and sent this train north, nonstop all the way to Grand Central Terminal."

Claire made a face.

"Are you a Catholic, Claire?" I asked.

"No. I'm an Episcopalian," said Claire.

I pictured Episcopal prayers as a lot lighter and bouncier than Catholic ones, but I didn't say so.

"Don't worry," I said. "I never heard of Episcopalian prayers getting people into trouble."

"I'll make it up to you, Oscar," said Claire. "I'll get Daddy to send you home on the real train to Chicago."

That was going to have to be the way it was. If I was lucky, I'd get back home all right, but it would be 1926 in Chicago, too. I'd be in kindergarten again. Eventually I'd have to live through the selling of our trains, Aunt Carmen's casseroles, and the robbers in the bank. Only after a while, I'd be none the wiser because I probably would forget the future the moment I began to live it over.

As the sun came up, Claire pointed out the window. A pleasant hill rose beside the train, its naked trees covered in dawn frost. "I think we are in western Pennsylvania," she said.

I had no idea, but within an hour, the train slowed again and the woodsy landscape around us thickened with villages and small cities.

"Claire, I have to prepare you for what is going to happen in New York. I'm going to be six years old again."

"C'mon, Oscar," she said.

"Claire, try to understand this. If you went in a rocket ship to the west and you flew over the international date line, you'd fly right into tomorrow. If you went east, you'd go into yesterday."

"I can't understand that stupid date line," said Claire. "It just zigs and zags right down the globe."

"Take it on faith then," I said. "They just made up that line, anyway. Listen, Lionel trains look like they're just running around a layout track. But they aren't. The minute you get on one, you run back and forth through time. California is two thousand miles to the west of where I got on, in Cairo. It gained me ten years. Chicago to New York is a thousand miles in the other direction. It'll lose me five years, and I'll be six years old."

"What are we going to do?" said Claire, after thinking this over.

"Be prepared," I said. "When we get to the edge of where the Lionel layout station ends, I'm going to hit a time pocket. There's no oxygen in a time pocket, just screaming noise and jelly air. It nearly choked me to death in Los Angeles. Just push me through it. Drag me through it."

"Will it happen to me, too?" asked Claire.

"Probably not. You never got off the train. You'll just be back in 1926, where you left, so there's no time pocket for you. Just me." I breathed in deeply. "I don't know how many of these I can do," I said.

"I'll get you through it, Oscar," said Claire. "I'm strong! When we get uptown, I'll have to sneak you into the apartment up the servants' stairs. We'll have to figure out a plan for after that, Oscar."

I whistled. "I'll be a first-grader without a penny to my name, separated from my dad by a thousand miles," I said. "And you, Claire! You're going to get holy heck in a handcar from your folks for running away. We're up a creek without a paddle!"

Claire sat very still on her bunk. *Clickety, clickety, clickety,* like an overworked metronome the train's wheels hummed on the track below us. She squinted thoughtfully. "We'd better stick together, Oscar," she said. "We are the only ones in the world who have ever done this train jumping."

Pennsylvania was as endless as Russia, but at last we hit New Jersey. The engine paused ever so slightly in a dirty yellow station called Newark. Then it sped on and entered a long tunnel. Within two minutes, it pulled into Grand Central Terminal, New York City, and it finally stopped, wheezing like a marathon runner.

The next thing I knew, Claire had me by the hand. "Come on, Oscar," she said. "Let's get out of here before they seal the doors."

Harry, the conductor, stood on the platform, hands on hips and feet planted wide. He opened his mouth in astonishment as we ran by. "Hey!" he yelled. "Hey! Youse! Come back here!" But Claire knew exactly where she was going. We melted away into the crowd of Grand Central.

"Where are we going?" I asked Claire.

"To the Lexington Avenue subway," she shouted. "Tell me when you hit that invisible wall, Oscar," said Claire, dodging right and left through the bustling crowd of commuters and travelers. Suddenly I couldn't move.

"Now!" I yelled. "I can't go any farther. I can't see it, Claire, but I can feel it! Can you?"

She could not. Claire was in her own time. Claire dashed back up behind me. She grabbed my hand in a vice grip and sidestepped a fat woman with two big shopping bags who was racing past. Claire shoved me in front of the woman. Behind her the woman's weight tumbled into us.

"My stars!" said the chubby woman. "Somebody needs to teach you some manners! Say excuse me!"

How Claire answered this, I did not know. The air around me had again turned thick and unbreathable. I heard only the clattering of a million marbles on a tin roof and then a popping sound from my own chest.

But I was through. Claire half-dragged me into a ceramic-tiled entranceway. The sign read 42ND ST. GR. CENTRAL in red mosaic just as it did on the Lionel layout stations. Claire tripped down the steps as if she owned them. I fell down the rest of the steps

after her and crumpled into a heap on the dirty stone floor. I lay in front of a newsstand underneath both Claire and the shopping lady.

"Is that you, Oscar?" Claire asked nervously, bending over to brush me off.

I could inhale only shallow gasps. Going through the barrier had cracked my ribs. I could no more run than someone in a head-to-toe plaster cast.

"Oscar?" asked Claire. "Is that you? I only see a little boy!"

"I'm in here," I managed to say. "I can't stand up."

Near my head was the spinner rack of the day's newspapers. I glanced at the *World-Telegram* and looked at the date. *"Christmas sales!"* it read. "December 31, 1926."

"Where are all of these people running to?" I panted. Old and young, tall and short, everyone galloped, up, down, and crosswise, in the echoing subway platforms. Briefcases banged against us. There were few *excuse me*'s from New Yorkers.

"It's the New York City subway at Grand Central. It's always like this," said Claire. "Even at midnight!"

Claire half carried me onto the IRT subway, which ran uptown to her home. I stumbled along beside her. The subway car lurched and heaved back and forth. "I'll just die," I whispered to Claire. "I'll just die right here. And now."

CHAPTER 15

I opened one eye and tried to figure out where I was. In a bed, that was for sure. I had only the vaguest memory of being put to bed. The Lexington Avenue subway had given my ribs such a pummeling, and the walk up ten flights of stairs was so painful that I had blubbered like a baby, stumbling from step to agonizing step. That much I recalled with vivid embarrassment.

But in bed I was quite comfortable. In Claire's apartment, the smell in the atmosphere was distinct and familiar. Through the air wafted the special scent of thick oriental carpets and lemon-oil furniture polish. Mixed in on top was the aroma of vanilla and butter cooking somewhere in a kitchen.

I ran my hand up and down my body gingerly to see how much it had been hurt. I discovered that my ribs were wrapped in tape. They felt better, snugger.

"Hello," said Claire. "Are you hungry, Oscar?"

I nodded and pulled myself carefully upright to lie back on two pillows. The pillows were as soft as two clouds.

Claire spooned me some very warm beef soup. Eating it brought strength back to me. She gave me two aspirin with a glass of milk. I could see almost nothing in the dark room. "Where are we, Claire?" I asked her when the soup was done, fingering the tape up and down my small rib cage.

"We're in a maid's room in our apartment house. We're on the third floor. Mummy and Daddy have a triplex. Nobody knows we're here, except Lisl, the maid. She won't talk because I gave her the Bonwit Teller gift certificate my granny gave me for Christmas. She's got New Year's Eve off. All the servants do. So no one's up here."

I did not ask Claire what a Bonwit Teller gift certificate was. "Your mother and father don't know you're home yet?" I asked. "Is the thirteen-state alarm still on for you?"

"Lisl told me it's still on," said Claire. "But we're safe. The cops have searched the whole apartment three times. They're standing downstairs in the lobby bored stiff. Mummy and Daddy are in the living room listening for the telephone to ring. We came up the servants' stairway. It's separate from the main lobby, so Bruno, the doorman, didn't see us." Claire took my soup bowl and spoon and set them on the floor.

"Who . . . who did this rib taping?" I asked.

"Oh," said Claire airily, "I did. I got out the *Boy Scout Handbook*. I figured you might have cracked ribs, and so I got the tape from my brother's Boy Scout kit and taped you up just the way the handbook says to do. Oscar," she said suddenly. Something was glinting in her hand. "What's this? I found it on a string around your neck with your religious medal when I taped you up." Claire held out my dime on a string.

"It's my dime on a string," I said. "Mr. Applegate

glued it on for me. We dropped it into the slot and ran the trains in the bank as much as we wanted."

"Oscar," she said cautiously as she handed the dime back to me, "this dime's from 1931. It's a genuine U.S. mint silver dime from five years into the future."

I was not surprised. I looked at Claire quizzically.

"Oscar. Can you get up out of bed?"

"I think so." Slowly I eased my aching body out from between the comfortable covers and pillows. The aspirin was helping. "What now?" I asked.

"Can you take this letter?" asked Claire. "Could you make it down the back stairway? It leads out the side door of the building. Then slip into the main lobby. Can you do that?"

"I think so, Claire. I'll try."

"Good! The cops are probably watching, but they won't be looking for a six-year-old boy. They won't even see you. Take this letter and put it in the mail-room basket at the back of the lobby." Claire looked at her watch. "The building superintendent brings up the mail three times a day. His next run's about ten minutes from now. Once drop the letter off, disappear quickly, Oscar. Whatever you do, don't call attention to yourself. Here's twenty cents. Outside the building, go left. On the avenue is a Schrafft's. Go in there."

"What's at Schrafft's?" I asked.

"Chicken salad sandwiches for my granny and her pals who shop and have lunch. And the best ice cream in New York," said Claire. "Sit at the counter and order a chocolate malted. And dawdle, Oscar. Take half an hour to drink it up. When you're finished, walk around the block and keep your eyes peeled for police hanging around. If the cops have left, go back to Bruno, the doorman. Make sure there's no policemen hanging around the lobby. Bruno should have a reply letter for you from Mummy and Daddy. Grab it. Make sure you're not followed. Then come back the way you came."

"Can I read what's in your letter first?" I asked.

"Of course!" said Claire.

The envelope was addressed to Mr. and Mrs. Robert W. Bister.

The letter had been written on Claire's own stationery. The words were block letters in red pen, straight and crisp as if lettered with a ruler.

DEAR MUMMY AND DADDY,

I HAVE NOT BEEN KIDNAPPED. I AM NEARBY IN THE CITY. I
WILL RETURN HOME SAFE AND SOUND IF YOU WILL SIGN THE
AGREEMENT BELOW. PLEASE TELL ALL THE POLICE TO GO
HOME. I AM FINE. PLEASE GIVE THE SIGNED AGREEMENT
IN AN ENVELOPE TO BRUNO, THE DOORMAN, RIGHT AWAY.
SOMEONE WILL COLLECT IT. IF THERE ARE NO POLICE
AROUND AND NO ONE FOLLOWS THAT PERSON, I WILL
APPEAR SOMETIME SOON AFTER THAT.

> LOVE, YR. DAUGHTER
> CLAIRE S. BISTER

I AGREE AND SOLEMNLY PROMISE, SO HELP ME GOD, THAT
CLAIRE, OUR DAUGHTER, WILL

A. NOT EVER BE SENT TO BOARDING SCHOOL OR HAVE A
   COMING OUT PARTY.
B. BE GIVEN NO MORE DOLLS AND SISSY CLOTHES AND
   BALLROOM DANCING LESSONS.
C. BE GIVEN THE ELECTRIC TRAIN OF HER CHOICE PLUS
   TRACK AND LAYOUT.

> SIGNED:
> EVELYN COMSTOCK BISTER _____
> ROBERT WHITNEY BISTER _____
> DATED _____ WITNESSED BY _____

SHOULD THIS AGREEMENT BE BREACHED OR IN ANY WAY
COMPROMISED, BE IT UNDERSTOOD BY ALL PARTIES THAT
CLAIRE S. BISTER WILL SHORTLY THEREAFTER VANISH IN
THE EXACT WAY SHE DID ON CHRISTMAS MORNING.

Claire gave me an old set of her brother's clothing, and I put them on. They fit better than the Bullock's clothes, which now hung on my peewee frame. I crept into the hallway and down the stairs. Every step felt like a kick from a mule.

There were three policemen, lollygagging around in the lobby. Claire was right about them not noticing me any more than they might have seen a fly buzzing by. I dropped her letter in a large wicker mail basket that stood in the middle of the mail room. The building was so swank that even the lobby smelled of melted butter and lilies.

Unseen, I glided out of the building, almost whistling, past Bruno, who was chatting with the police about the Dodgers' chances in the coming baseball season. No one even looked up. I strolled two doors down and saw the big red and white sign, Schrafft's. I had never been to a restaurant and ordered by myself, even when I was eleven. Would they laugh at me or throw me out? I sat at the counter. It was not too different from the counter in Mr. Kinoshura's drugstore, where Dad and I used to go for sodas together, except my feet didn't touch the footrest on the stool. Brave as I could sound, I ordered a chocolate malted.

"You're awfully young to be ordering in a restaurant, honey," said the waitress a little doubtfully.

Would she call the police and turn me in somewhere? My forehead began to sweat at the thought. "My mother's coming to meet me," I explained. "She's just doing some shopping and then she's coming right along."

The waitress brought my soda and set it down on a paper doily in front of me. "There you are! Now, sip it slowly," she chirruped. Then she took my napkin and tucked it in under my chin for me.

"May I ask the time, ma'am?" I said politely.

"Of course!" said the waitress. She took off her wristwatch so I could see it. "Now, that's the big hand and that's the little hand. Do you know what the big hand and the little hand say?"

"I beg your pardon, ma'am?" I said.

"Can you count yet?" she asked with a smile. "Can you tell time?"

"Count? I can do long division and fractions," I answered.

"But you can't be more than five years old," she said.

"Don't call attention to yourself, Oscar!" Claire's warning came flooding back.

I put my twenty cents on the counter, hoping to distract the waitress. She brought me five cents in change. "One, two, three, four, five pennies!" she said merrily.

"Keep the change, ma'am," I mumbled.

But the waitress looked at me even more curiously than before and slyly checked the door to see if my mother was coming in for me.

Happily for me, church bells down the block tolled the half hour. Outside, on Park Avenue, two police car sirens went off. The patrol cars sped past Schrafft's big front window on their way downtown. Their sirens faded in the noise of the traffic outside. I squirmed off my counter seat and sidled out the door before the waitress could ask me any more questions about my mother.

I ambled casually past the entrance of Claire's building. No cops in sight. I checked across the street, peering into corner phone booths and parked cars. No cops. I cleared the whole of the block and then moseyed into the lobby of the building. There were no cops anywhere, allowing me to trot right up to Bruno. "Letter for Miss Claire Bister, please," I said.

Bruno seemed to go into shock. "But you're only a—"

I snatched the letter out of his hand and scooted back out through the revolving glass door before he could say anything more. Then I disappeared into the side entrance, where the servants' stairway let out. No one had followed me. I bolted up the steps as fast as my aching ribs would let me.

I collapsed onto the bed. "I'm not moving again today," I groaned.

Claire opened the letter. "Aha!" she said. "I knew they'd sign! I won! They agreed to everything! Oscar, I'm going downstairs now. If you want to hear what happens, go to the laundry chute outside in the hall, open it up, and listen!"

I heard very little except the echo of the laundry chute itself for a few minutes. Suddenly a woman's voice shrieked. Claire's mother, no question about it. A man's deep baritone, her father, started hallooing and hooting and slapping something that sounded like leather. They all started singing, "For she's a jolly good fellow!" There was great happiness on Claire's arrival, that was certain. Claire's family might be a little slow on the uptake about their daughter, but they didn't sound like totally bad parents to me.

"Where were you, darling?" asked her mother over and over again when the dust had settled.

"Out and about!" said Claire. "Here and there!"

"Were you abducted?" asked her father sternly. "Were you kidnapped?"

"No," said Claire. "I never actually left the apartment."

Her mother managed a laugh like bells tinkling. "Darling," she said, "you can have any Christmas present you want, and we'll never send you to boarding school. You can go right here in town to Brearley School! Or The Spence School! Any school you want!"

Mrs. Bister's trilling voice sounded eerily like Mrs. Pettishanks. It was an accent. Actors and actresses used that English-y accent in the movies, too.

"I want to go to plain old public school," said Claire. "P.S. 6. It's perfectly good."

Mr. and Mrs. Bister met this request with

silence. I reckoned they would never spring for public school, but they would also not argue about it now. And they wouldn't talk about the coming-out party either, since it was seven years off. They'd hope Claire would change. I knew she wouldn't.

Someone brought food in to Claire. I could hear the clink of silver and glassware.

"After lunch," Claire said, "I'd like to go over to FAO Schwarz if it's okay with you."

"Anything you want, darling," her father chimed in. "We'll go together! Name it. You can have three train sets! Just don't disappear on us again."

"Thank God the police are gone, dear," said Claire's mother clearly to Claire's father. "Their uniforms smelled like donkeys! We should write the police department and tell them to provide showers for their officers and send those uniforms to the dry cleaners."

"You sound like a socialist, dear!" teased Mr. Bister good-naturedly.

What was a socialist? I think I remembered that Aunt Carmen had used the word to describe darkly clad people who didn't go to church and met in basements to overthrow the government.

As the Bisters' lunch progressed, I lost interest in their chatter and went back to bed. I fell back against my pillows gratefully. I was happy for Claire. She was going to get her train at last. But my heart was as cold as a stone inside me. How would I ever get back to Cairo? Would I ever see my dad again and hear his gravelly, comforting laugh? Would I ever cook him dinner again or watch him light up one of his cigars? I drew the pillow over my head and said ten Hail Marys for deliverance, but if anyone in heaven heard them, they were lost in the shuffle.

It was then that the telephone downstairs began to ring.

It rang and rang and no one answered. Did that mean the house was empty? Wouldn't a stray servant answer it? It was New Year's Eve afternoon. Claire said the servants had the day off.

Twelve unanswered rings. A sneaky voice inside me nibbled like a mouse. It whispered, "Oscar, how about calling your dad on the Bisters' telephone! It's New Year's Eve, and he's probably home." I stopped myself. *Don't trouble trouble, Oscar!* I warned myself. But I didn't listen. Our Cairo telephone number was stitched into my heart.

My ribs, too, screamed at me to stay put. None-theless I got up and crept into the hallway. Not a sound greeted me. The entrance through the servants' quarters to the apartment down below was in front of me. I went through the doorway.

Better not risk it, I argued with myself as I slid snakelike, one bare foot after another, down the stairs to the main rooms of the Bisters' apartment.

Like fingers, my toes grasped the carpet beneath. I could have heard a feather flutter to the floor, the house was so quiet. Supposing I ran into Claire's brother? Was he hanging around somewhere? I didn't want to think about him.

Careful, Oscar. Still plenty of time to turn around and go back to bed! Go back where it's safe! Do it now! I instructed myself in an inner yell. But again I did not listen to a word I said. The possibility of my dad's "Hello!" along the telephone wires was too great a pull.

I found myself on the bedroom level. Oil paintings in heavy gilt frames lined the walls. One of those oriental runners caressed my feet, its red and blue silk patterns comforting to my little boy's toes. To my right was the Bisters' master bedroom. Next to their four-poster lay a polar bear rug with the bear's head, teeth bared, still intact. I shuddered, picturing the poor bear, its life ended cruelly — not to mention having its beautiful thick pelt walked on by Mrs. Bister's dainty feet morning and night. I looked on the bedside table. No telephone in sight. Where would these people have their telephone? Probably just like the Pettishankses, and other rich River Heights families, the Bisters had a telephone room.

Where would the Bisters' telephone room be? On the ground floor, of course. Even more dangerous. I inched down the next set of stairs.

The parlor, if that's what the Bisters called it, was as big as the entire floor of our house on Lucifer Street. It looked out over a snow-covered park two blocks away. Bulky wing chairs, embroidered with silk dragonflies, guarded either side of the marble fireplace. The hearth was immaculate and laid with small logs, stacked with military precision. I was tempted to jump on a creamy velvet sofa, but kept walking. No telephone here. I reckoned the sofa alone could fit five people. Count in the beefy leather easy chairs, and the room could hold two dozen comfortably, without bringing in wooden folding chairs from the garage, like my dad always did when Thanksgiving was at our house.

They don't have wooden folding chairs. They don't have a garage! I reminded myself. One of the Bisters' overstuffed ottomans could no doubt pay for all our Sears Roebuck furniture back in Cairo.

Go back, Oscar! the inner voice urged me. *Just one minute to hear Dad say hello. That's all I want,* I bargained with that unreasonable other Oscar.

A pair of French doors at the end of the parlor opened into the dining room. A dozen ladder-back chairs with gold inlay at the joints were precisely spaced around a mahogany table, its surface polished like a mirror. Overhead hung a chandelier with a hundred glass dangles on it.

Thankfully, the room to the side of this one was indeed the Bisters' telephone room. It was decorated in the Spanish style. Heavy wine-colored draperies hung over the windows. Gold-thread dragonflies were embroidered into the velvet. I turned the lamp on. The light blazed through spangled colored panes, each no bigger than my thumbnail. Another dragon-fly design — the Bisters must have liked dragonflies. Overlooking the telephone itself was an ivory statuette of a Greek god holding a snake-entwined staff. He had silver wings coming out of his heels.

"Mercury, Oscar!" I could almost hear Mrs. Olderby's voice reminding me. When Mrs. Olderby taught us ancient history, she made sure we memorized the names and characteristics of every god in Greek, Roman, and Egyptian heaven.

Glued in a tiny window on the front of the phone was the Bisters' number, BUtterfield 8-7053. I picked up the receiver.

"Number, please?" said the operator. Immediately I was cheered by her voice, and my fears subsided. She was every bit as nice-sounding as the operators in Cairo, and she was going to put me through to my dad.

"Cairo, Illinois, please, ma'am. Cairo-six, oh-eight-four-five," I repeated. My heart quickened inside me. *Just hello—that's all I want to hear!* I told myself. *Then I'll hang up and run back to the room and no one will see me and I'll be safe. I promise!*

"Illinois?" asked the operator. "Did you say Illinois, honey?"

"Yes," I answered, trying to lower my six-year-old voice. There was that name *honey* again.

"Sweetie-pie," piped the operator primly. "Bell Telephone operators are not allowed to accept long-distance calls placed by children."

"I'm eleven," I pleaded.

"Is there some grown-up at home who can make this call for you?" asked the operator.

"No!" I said.

"That's what I thought," said the operator. "Children like to play jokes over the telephone, so the company won't take kiddy calls long distance. Now go and find your mommy or poppy, and then you can ask them to call long distance. Okay? Happy New Year!"

All this for nothing! my inner voice croaked. *Scram, Oscar, while the scramming is good!* Held-back tears of disappointment throbbed in my jaw muscles. I hung up the receiver and wiped the prints off the telephone with the tail of one of the drapes. Back through the dining room I went, this time at a trot, which is all my burning ribs would allow, back through the parlor with its mighty chairs and lacquered tables, and upward I padded on the first stairway to the bedroom level.

As my foot reached the top step, a key turned in

the front-door latch and the bolt clicked back. I scampered upward, heart hammering as the room below me filled with happy voices. My adventure with the phone had made me a nervous wreck. On Lisl's dresser was a bottle of Nervosa. The label claimed to clear the bloodstream of clot-forming anxieties. I swallowed a big gulp and waited for it to take effect. After a time Claire reappeared. She beckoned to me from the doorway. "C'mon, Oscar!" she said.

"Where to?" I asked.

"My room! Mummy and Daddy have guests for tea downstairs," said Claire. "They won't come up again. Wait'll you see the train, Oscar! I got the biggest, best layout I could find!"

"It's the Twentieth Century, Claire!" I nearly shouted when I got to Claire's room and saw the engine. The Twentieth Century Express ran regular service from New York to Chicago. Claire's layout came with two terminals, New York's Grand Central and Chicago's Union Station.

We ran the train back and forth, blew the whistle, and put smoke into its stack. "Are you happy, Claire?" I asked, glancing at her eyes. Her dreamy eyes did not look happy. "What's the matter?" I asked, crouching in front of her in the middle of the oval of newly laid railroad tracks. "You have to be thrilled about this train! It's what you wanted, Claire! If you asked 'em, they'd probably buy you three more!"

Claire looked down at the train. "I don't want you to leave and go home, Oscar," Claire said. "But I won't be happy until you're happy and that means when you get safely home. You see, you're the first person in the whole wide world I've ever really truly cared about, Oscar."

"Me?"

"Yes, Oscar. You."

I felt myself blush as red as a Lionel signal flare. "You love your mother and dad, too!" I said. "Not to mention your brother, wherever he is."

"I love them, of course, Oscar. But no one's ever listened to me like you and taken me seriously before you. Now you have to go home, and I don't want you to go."

"But how?" I asked. "I can't jump onto your train, Claire. There's nothing to scare me back onto it. Nothing can make me jump onto this layout and take me back to 1931 where I belong."

"I'll get Daddy to pay for a real ticket on a real train," said Claire.

"Your dad won't be happy to find a strange little boy in his apartment. The wrong kind of boy, too!" I added.

Claire took a deep breath. "If we play our cards right, Oscar, we can get you home tonight."

I sighed. "It's better than nothing, Claire," I said. "But back in Cairo I'll still be a kindergartener. And then in five years' time, Dad'll lose his job again. We'll have to sell our trains all over again. And Mr. Applegate will be shot dead again."

"No, he won't!" said Claire. "I'll think of something!" She frowned. A hundred ideas were scampering around in Claire's brain. I could almost see them like eggs scrambling in a frying pan.

"First things first, Oscar," she said. "If you go back home to Cairo with some money in a bank account, your dad will never have to sell your house. You'll never move in with your aunt Carmen, and Mr. Applegate won't ever get shot."

"But how are you going to do that, Claire? It'd take a small fortune to buy back our house."

She thumped a code on the far wall of her room. *Thumpety-thump-thump . . . thump, thump.*

There was a return *thump.* "Good!" said Claire. "He's home."

"Who's that?" I asked.

"It's my brother," said Claire. "Poor Max. He's in the boys' choir. He had to spend the whole day down in Saint Thomas's Church on Fifth Avenue scrubbing the statuary with a toothbrush and Bon Ami."

"What? Why?"

"Last Sunday he was caught spitting in the choir stall at evensong. He and the other boys have spitting contests. The choirmaster's very strict. The boys hate scrubbing the saints' feet, but they keep spitting anyway. Max has a singing voice like an angel. He gets solos. Otherwise they wouldn't let him back in the choir again and again."

At the door stood a grumpy-looking fifth-grade boy in one of those sailor blouses that all the country club boys in River Heights wore when they got dressed up. His hands were an irritated nasty color, blotchy pink all the way up to the wrists.

He asked, "Who's this midget? He's wearing my clothes too! Stop looking at my hands, midget!"

"This is my brother, Maxwell, Oscar," said Claire. "Max, meet Oscar."

"Who the heck is this little squirt?" asked Max.

"Your twin?" I asked Claire.

"Yup," said Claire, looking him up and down. "Not identical in any way!"

Max wiped his nose on the sleeve of his shirt and stared at me with contempt. "Why are you here? You look like something the cat dragged in," he said.

"My name is Oscar Ogilvie. I am eleven years old and I come from Cairo, Illinois," I answered him.

"Yer six. Not a day older," said Maxwell. "Yer a twerp! Those clothes don't even fit." He sniffed at me. "Look at yer front teeth, for the love of God!"

My hand flew to cover my mouth. My two front teeth were missing, leaving a wide gap.

"Max," said Claire, "Oscar comes from the year 1931, where he will be eleven. He's six outside, but he's eleven inside."

"Prove it," said Maxwell, pouting.

"Show the dime to him, Oscar," said Claire.

With great reluctance, I handed my dime to Maxwell, keeping hold of the end of the string.

"Look at the date, fathead," said Claire.

"Jesus, Mary, and Joseph!" said Maxwell. "Howdja get that, twerp?"

"Shut up, Max," said Claire. "I want you to do me a favor."

"Depends what it is, and it'll cost you," said Max.

"You can have the dime for one hour, Max. Give it to your friend Henry. Ask him to show it to his father."

"Who's Henry?" I asked.

"His best friend," said Claire. "Then bring it right back to Oscar, Max. If you lose it, I'll kill you. Okay? Swear to God and hope to die with a poison stake in your heart if you don't bring that dime right back. And don't tell anyone Oscar's here."

"Supposing I don't want to," said Max.

"If you don't do it, Max, I'll tell Mummy and Daddy that you and Henry went up to the penthouse and lit a fire and roasted marshmallows on the roof."

"You wouldn't tell!" said Max heatedly.

"I would too."

Max considered this. "I told you it'll cost you,"

said Max, staring at the dime, which was now in the palm of his hand.

"What'll it cost me?" asked Claire.

Max looked up, calculating. "I have three book reports due next month. No less than ten pages each," he said. "*Last of the Mohicans, Ivanhoe, Red Badge of Courage.*"

"Deal," said Claire.

"Plus your Christmas chocolate Santa," Max added.

"Deal!" said Claire. "Now move your tootsies. No telling anybody. Swear to God and hope to die."

"Swear to God," said Max. Max left the room with my dime in his back pocket and no more to say.

"Do you trust him?" I asked Claire.

"Of course not!" said Claire. "But he'll show that dime to Henry, all right, and Henry'll show it to his old man. Henry's dad is a coin collector. Henry Mellon Senior'll put the dime under a big magnifier, and he'll be on the phone to Daddy in three minutes' time. It's just what I want!"

"Why?" I asked.

"Oscar," said Claire. "Think hard. Remember all that stuff you told me on the train about the crash?"

"The crash? The Wall Street crash in 1929?"

"Oscar, please, please try to remember everything you ever knew or heard about that crash and about why the millionaires jumped out their windows and why the banks closed and all that."

"Oh, Claire," I moaned, "I don't know anything."

"You know enough," said Claire. "You lived through it!"

We sent the Twentieth Century around dozens more loops until we heard a squeak on a stair floorboard. A heavy foot approached us, heavier certainly than Max's.

There was a knock on the door. A firm, no-nonsense knock that meant only a few seconds would pass before the handle turned and whoever it was would come in, anyway.

Chapter 16

"Who is this, Claire?" asked Robert W. Bister. Her father was a splendid, in-the-pink kind of man with center-parted hair and a tweed suit that no one in Cairo could buy, even in the Cairo department store. He squatted in a friendly way on the carpet in front of me and bounced a bit on his tweed-covered haunches and his gleaming leather cordovans.

"This is Oscar, Dad," said Claire. "Oscar Ogilvie Junior of Cairo, Illinois."

Mr. Bister shook my little hand solemnly and with respect. "Is this yours, Oscar?" asked Claire's father. He held out my dime.

"Yes, sir," I answered, plucking the coin with caution from his outstretched hand.

"Claire, darling," said her father, his eyes still on me, as if I might somehow escape, "I am afraid we cannot harbor missing children in our home. It is against the law, and your mother and I could be arrested."

"I'm not a missing child, sir," I said.

"You've got to be missing from somewhere," her father said reasonably. "You're five years old, and somebody must own you!" He smiled at his little joke.

"I'm eleven years old, sir," I said. "I live at number three, Lucifer Street, Cairo, Illinois. I am in Mrs. Olderby's fifth grade at Cairo Central School. Normally I am four feet five inches tall, and I am here of my own accord."

"How did you get here, Oscar?" he asked in a very friendly tone.

"You'll never believe him, Dad," snapped Claire. "It would be a waste of breath for Oscar to go through the whole story."

Her father changed tack. He tossed the empty Lionel boxes onto the floor from the easy chair where Claire had put them and took a seat. "That coin," he said, pointing to it. "Max showed it to Henry. Henry thought the dime was a fake and showed it to his father. Henry's father happens to be an ace amateur numismatist. That means he's a coin collector. He examined this Liberty dime under a special magnifier. It's absolutely genuine. Sterling silver. Nobody forges trick coins with real silver. It even has a mint mark in the corner. Unfakeable. I want to know how you got here, Oscar Ogilvie, and how you came by that dime."

"You promise not to interrupt and make fun, Dad?" prodded Claire.

"Scout's honor, my dear," said her father, and he crossed his tweed-swathed legs and beady-eyed me over his folded fingers.

I began with the trains in our basement on Lucifer Street. From there I went to news of the crash in our morning paper, and the rich men jumping out of windows and selling apples in the street. Then to my dad losing his job, Mr. Pettishanks's bank taking our house, Mr. Applegate's visits, and Aunt Carmen. I told him about Stackpole and McGee, about my first jumping onto the train and about Dutch meeting me on the Rock Island Line. All the while Mr.

Bister absorbed it like blotting paper. He nodded his head frequently.

I described the Crawford layout. And then it happened.

I forgot Miss Chow's name. It mattered frighteningly to me. It meant the forgetting was beginning. It meant that in this little boy's body, five years in the past, I was already forgetting the future. I had to leave 1926 and get back to my own time and my own eleven-year-old body or even Mr. H. and Dutch would all go up in smoke. Then I would be none the wiser for all I had gone through.

"Miss Chow," interjected Claire. "You said her name was Miss Chow."

"Of course," I stammered, and went on smoothly, describing Mr. H. and his bassett-hound face, "Hizzy" Hissbaum, and Lieutenant Cyril Pettishanks sending me to fight the Krauts with the Russkies. Mr. Bister stopped me there.

"War?" he asked. "What war? When?"

"I don't know, exactly," I answered. "I came in December 1941. Japan had just attacked America in a place called Pearl something. The whole world was in the army."

Claire stopped me with a gentle finger on the top of my hand. "Daddy," she said, "as you can see, Oscar has to get home. He has to get back to his real life."

"Oscar, I'll make a bargain with you," said Claire's father.

"Dad, you're such a lawyer!" said Claire.

"And you, my dear?" he asked with a gleeful smile. "Did you not only this afternoon strike up a very good bargain with your mother and me? And, may I add, in perfectly square legal terms!"

Claire had to admit that was true.

Pride swam in her father's voice. "I am indeed a famous lawyer, dear girl. But then we are a lawyer's family. You make deals, Max makes deals, and I make deals. Deals make the world go round. I, personally, would sign a contract with Mussolini himself to find out what is going to happen to all our family investments in the year 1929. I don't want to be jumping out of any high windows. It would upset your mother to no end if I did!" He laughed at his own joke.

Mr. Bister's eyes didn't miss a trick. "I saw a flicker of recognition at the word *Mussolini*," he said to me.

Mussolini . . . Who was Mussolini? I pricked my brain from all sides. "He was the leader of the Italians, in the war," I said.

"Oscar," said Mr. Bister seriously, "you spill everything you remember about what happens in 1929 to my friends and colleagues, and I will send you home with a first-class ticket on any train you like. A real, live train this time, Oscar. There's one that leaves in a few hours. Deal?"

I looked at Claire. She was shaking her head ever so slightly at me and studying her father. Jumbled possibilities raced through my mind. If I went home on a real train, I'd be doomed to repeat everything I'd lived through and I'd be doomed to repeat everything I'd done. But if I said no, how would I ever get home? My heart turned over inside me at the bleak choice.

"Hold on a second, Daddy," said Claire.

"What could be better than that, dear girl?" interrupted her dad. He kept me in the corner of his sight.

Claire went on: "It's fine to send Oscar back on the train, Daddy. But we'll have to give him some money, too. That way he and his father will be able to keep their house when the crash comes and his dad won't ever have to leave Oscar for California."

"How much was your house worth, son?" Mr. Bister asked. "How about five thousand? Will that do it? A money order for five thousand in your pocket?"

My jaw dropped open.

"Make it ten, Daddy," said Claire.

"Seventy-five hundred," said her father. "But, Claire . . ."

"But what?" asked Claire.

"This lad's information better be good," added Mr. Bister. "He'd better pass the test and give us the inside dope or the deal's off."

I shuddered at the idea of passing a test. What would it be? Claire saw me go a little pale.

"No deal, Daddy," she said, crossing her arms on her chest and walking away to the other side of the room.

I began to panic. This was my only chance. Was Claire going to blow it?

"What do you mean, my lovely?" asked her father.

"Oscar isn't passing any tests. Pay up square for whatever Oscar can remember and tells you he remembers. He'll do his best. If you don't agree, Oscar never heard of the word *crash*."

Mr. Bister twiddled both sets of fingers inside his

jacket pockets. "And if your young friend is a fake?" he asked. "If he lies or humiliates me in front of my business colleagues?"

Claire narrowed her eyes. "Oscar doesn't lie, Daddy," she said. "And he's no phoney!"

"If he isn't the real McCoy, my darling," said her father, "if he makes me look like a fool, the deal's off. I won't pay good money for wooden nickels."

Claire held out her hand to her father. "Deal," she said. "But remember, Daddy, Oscar's only eleven and he hasn't read the *Wall Street Journal* every day of his life, like you."

"Deal," said her father. "You're a toughie, Claire. You'll be the first girl to sit on the Supreme Court someday. Don't tell your mother I said so or she'll have a heart attack."

It was my impression from the smile he tried to hide that Mr. Bister had, himself, tutored Claire in bargaining skills. I also would lay bets that Maxwell had none of these talents. An hour later firm hands guided me to the doorway. "Now, Oscar, will you kindly come down into the living room? On very short notice I have decided to assemble a circle of my closest friends."

I followed him down the stairs, Claire close at hand behind me. She pulled me back toward her on the landing and whispered to me, "Be good, Oscar. Be really good and try to tell these men what they want to know."

"What will they want to know?" I asked.

"They are very wealthy men," said Claire, "and they will want you to tell them how they can stay rich and maybe even get a little richer."

"But what do I know?" I asked.

"Oscar, you know 1931. You know 1941, too. Daddy's friends want to figure out how to avoid that crash. They'll want to know ahead of time what that war is about so they can take their money out of German and Japanese investments."

"But I don't know anything about investments!" I whispered. "I don't even understand why your mother'd have a heart attack if you got to be the first lady on the Supreme Court."

"Because no man would marry me, silly!" said Claire. She poked me between the shoulder blades. "Be good, Oscar!" she said, and goosed me down-stairs into the Bisters' parlor.

Spread out around a cheery fire were five very

important-looking men. No Cairo Shoe Emporium brogans on their feet. Their gleaming wingtips had the slim leather soles of men who walked on marble floors. No broken fingernails or calluses on their hands. Their fingers were soft to the touch, nails pink and polished, as only comes when you don't use your hands for work. Each smiling mouth contained dazzling teeth. No dentures there. They were tycoons, every one, and they were beautiful to behold. There was no other word for it. Power oozed into the air around them.

"This is Henry's father, Henry Mellon Senior," said Mr. Bister. "He's the coin collector. You may have heard of his family."

I had not heard of it. But Henry Mellon was dressed so finely, his shave and haircut so barber-perfect, that I guessed he might not even put on his own socks in the morning but had someone to do it for him.

I was introduced to Mr. John P. Morgan and a Mr. Biddle. Next was a young man in a tennis sweater with wavy hair named Nelson Rockefeller. Then came a Joe Kennedy, who was accompanied by his son, who couldn't have been more than ten.

There were more freckles on young Kennedy than on a patch of gravel and he had the thickest thatch of hair I'd ever seen. The boy took no notice of me. His eyes flicked on me a second and he yawned. Last were a Mr. Merrill and Mr. Lynch, who sat together on a love seat. They all gave off a smell of butter and bay rum.

I guessed they mostly were bankers and such because they had that Pettishanks smell and they sat in the Pettishanks positions with their legs crossed, just so.

"Hi, Oscar!" Mr. Biddle greeted me heartily and each of the men shook my little six-year-old hand. It was Mr. Mellon who cleared his throat and began to speak. "This Liberty dime of yours, Oscar . . ." He smiled encouragingly at me. "I have an amateur darkroom. I've run off a photographic enlargement of the coin." Mr. Mellon handed me a black and white picture of my dime enlarged twentyfold. "See that mark near the rim?"

"Yes, sir."

"That's a mint mark. Only the federal mint has the capacity to create a mint mark. The ridges around the rim of the coin are unmistakable. Forgers can never get the ridges evenly. It isn't worth a forger's time to forge a dime, anyway. So, what we have here is a sterling silver United States mint coin of a series not yet in circulation, from a year that has not yet happened. Where did you get it?"

"From the night watchman at the First National Bank in Cairo, Illinois, sir. We used to run the Christmas train display with it," I answered. "It's glued to a string so we could yank it out of the coin slot and reuse it."

"And that was when, Oscar?"

"About mid-December 1931."

"And you are a boy from that time. Is that correct, Oscar?"

"Yes, sir. I was born in 1920, and I am eleven years old."

A chuckle went through the room and a shifting of legs in the comfortable upholstery.

"Eleven?" asked Mr. Rockefeller. "Is there anything you can tell us to convince us of that, Oscar?"

"I can probably do a long division problem for you if you want," I said. "I can do fractions, if they're not too hard." The young Kennedy boy yawned again and mouthed the word *show-off* at me silently.

"That won't be necessary, Oscar," said Claire's father. I took my seat at Claire's side. "Your questions, gentlemen?" he asked with a certain smugness, as if he, himself, had invented me.

"Who's the president of the United States in 1931, son?" asked Mr. Biddle.

"Herbert Hoover, sir," I answered.

"Good man, Hoover!" said several of the men, nodding.

"Oh, no, sir," I injected. "Mr. Hoover let the country go into a terrible mess after 1929, and he didn't know how to get out of it. Hoover fiddled while Rome burned. That's what my dad said, anyway. Do you want to know who the movie stars will be?"

"Your dad is probably a Democrat," huffed Mr. Merrill.

"Oh, yes, sir." I looked at their frightened faces. "I could tell you about the cars! The cars in 1941 are amazing. They will look like rockets compared to today." I wanted to tell them about Dutch's Thunderbolt and the color movies. "Joe DiMaggio of the Yankees will hit fifty home runs and steal seventy-six bases in 1941," I said, thinking about what had interested my dad, but they did not want to know about Joe DiMaggio.

"You say there is going to be a war in 1941?" asked Mr. Bister.

"Yes, sir. With the Japanese. They will attack us. The Germans will be back in it, too, and the Russians. There will be a new president, but I can't remember his name."

"Try, Oscar," encouraged Mr. Lynch.

I toed the pattern of the Turkish carpet. His name had disappeared. I couldn't make it come back. I shook my head and said, "My dad voted for him twice."

"Can you tell us what happened in the year 1929? Everything you remember from the newspapers and the radio."

"It was in the fall," I answered. "October '29." I tried beefing up my piping five-year-old voice without success. "There was a crash somewhere right here in New York City on Wall Street. That caused what they called a depression. Businessmen lost all their money and jumped out of windows and other ones had to sell their diamond stud pins and hawk apples on street corners."

The men looked at one another.

"What stocks were affected? Can you remember?" asked Mr. Bister.

"Stocks?" I asked.

"Well, how did Standard Oil do? Did it lose money?" asked Mr. Rockefeller.

"How about municipal bonds?" said Mr. Bister. "And General Electric? Did General Electric survive?"

"What about General Motors?" asked Mr. Mellon.

"Everything crashed," I answered. "The banks began to close. Everyone except the really, really rich people in the country was poor. The factories closed, and there were no jobs. Farmers couldn't farm because of dust storms."

It was then that I saw the tycoons' true purpose. Sitting around the Bisters' fireplace were the very profiteers that Mr. Applegate and Aunt Carmen had talked about. They might as well have asked me who would win next year's Kentucky Derby. All they wanted to do was get hot tips and make more money than ever, farmers and factory workers be d——d.

"And just what caused this crash, Oscar, d'ya

know?" asked Mr. Biddle, crossing his legs and plucking his trousers, just so. "What led up to it?"

I remembered what Aunt Carmen had said. "Margin calls!" I answered. I pulled in a deep breath and repeated Aunt Carmen's words. "Whatever margin calls are, and greed. Greedy Wall Street profiteers, gambling more than they were worth and building a house of cards until it all crashed down around their ears. They were like fortune-tellers at the horse races. I guess that's why they called it the crash."

There was an uncomfortable silence in the Bister living room, clear shifting around on the cushions of the chairs, and muttering.

Mr. Kennedy had a distinct way of talking. "Boy," he said, forgetting my name, "who'd you say was president after Mistah Hoovah? Who was it?"

I closed my eyes. *Who was that? Oh, yes! That was it. The same name as President Theodore Roosevelt.* "Frank. Franklin. It's Franklin Roosevelt."

"Franklin Roosevelt!" The name seemed to slingshot around the room.

"Are you sure of that, Oscar?" asked Mr. Bister.

"Yes," I said. "He won twice. I saw a picture of

him on a magazine cover. He was standing on an aircraft carrier saluting hundreds of sailors."

Mr. Merrill cleared his throat and clinked the ice cubes in his drink. "Boy?" he addressed me.

"Yes, sir."

"Do you know what polio is?"

"No, sir."

"I didn't think so. Polio is what Frank Roosevelt has. He's flat on his back in a bed. There's no cure for it, and if you get it you never walk again. Frank Roosevelt's never going to stand on an aircraft carrier. He'll never run for president or anything else again for the rest of his life! That bucktoothed wife of his'd never let 'im do it, anyway. President Franklin Roosevelt, my eye!"

Claire's father turned on me. His face was concerned. "I think you're mistaken about that, son," he said. "There is no way in the world that Frank Roosevelt will ever be president. Not with polio. I don't believe you saw him standing up on an aircraft carrier either."

There were humphs and mutterings in the room.

"And I am not so darned sure you're eleven years old, either."

My stomach clenched at his tone.

"Oscar!" Claire broke in. "Do 'If' for them. No six-year-old could recite 'If.' Just do it!"

The judgment of the men in the room was still suspended. Cigars and cigarettes were lit.

"Go ahead!" said Claire's father. "Make me believe in you, Oscar."

I stood in the middle of the hearth rug and began. "If you can . . . if you can make a heap—no, wait . . . wait. If you can keep your head when . . . when all about you are blaming you—no, wait . . ." I felt my pulse race as the words to Kipling's poem, always as familiar as my own fingernails, wilted in my mind and disappeared. Claire's face fell. I was forgetting. The future was dropping away from my mind, perhaps to be lost forever.

"Come on, Oscar!" said Claire. "You can do it in your sleep!" Claire began to mouth the words as I had once done for Cyril. But it was no good. I stumbled worse than Cyril had ever done. The poem had vanished from my mind like a star in the morning sky.

"An out-and-out little fakah! A liah!" commented Mr. Kennedy. "President Frank Roosevelt!

What a joke! Greedy profitee-ahs, indeed. I'm no greedy profitee-ah!"

Claire rounded on him. "Oscar's an all-American, Midwestern boy who goes to church on Sundays. He's told you the truth, Mr. Kennedy, but I don't think anyone in the room wants to hear the truth! Everybody here just wants to make more and more money!"

"You are faking, Oscar, if that's even your real name," said Mr. Bister to me calmly. "And lying. I can tell a liar by his eyes." He turned to Claire. "Deal's off, young lady!" he said, and tossed my dime onto the hearth rug at my feet. "Probably got this from some street magician!" he snapped.

Claire didn't argue. She took my hand and glared at Mr. Kennedy, his son, and both Mr. Merrill and Mr. Lynch. "Come on, Oscar, we'll go upstairs."

Mr. Bister was not going to give me a plug nickel. I knew that much. Claire and I plodded up the stairs in silence.

We heard someone say, "What are you going to do with this scruffy little orphan?"

"I'll have to call my lawyer," said Claire's father.

"Dammit, Bistah! You ahra lawyah!" Mr. Kennedy chimed in with his flat and nasal tones.

Claire said not very much at all, but her eyes spoke and I knew what was in them. I had made her father look like a fool in front of his friends, and I'd blown the whole thing. We sat in her window seat and looked down at the traffic on Seventieth Street without speaking. Supper had been prepared and sat on a silver tray on her table, but neither of us had any appetite for it. Claire found me a pair of Max's old Brooks Brothers pajamas and a toothbrush. Suddenly she touched my arm and said, "Let's listen in!"

Claire pulled down the laundry chute's iron handle and put nearly half her head into the opening. A draft of chilly air wafted up through the chute and with it, the voices. We listened to Claire's mother and father talking over supper.

We heard their knives and forks clinking on their dinner plates. We heard the squeak of furniture as they moved in their chairs. They gabbed away about the parties they would attend and the ones they would not bother with and the friends who might or might not attend each. At last Mrs. Bister hiccupped. Then she said, "Robert, what are we going to do with the little runaway upstairs?"

"I was going to send him back where he came

from on a train," answered Claire's father, mouth full of something. "But he might come back."

"You can't send him on a train alone like a piece of baggage," Mrs. Bister argued. "The railway requires adult accompaniment, and we are not going all the way to Chicago with that little urchin."

The word *urchin* stung me like a wasp. But she went on and we listened intently. "I've tried to reach the father in . . . where is it he said he's from? Cairo, Illinois. No listing whatever under Ogilvie," countered Claire's father.

My breath stopped short. Of course there was no listing! It was 1926. Dad didn't get us a telephone until 1928, two years later. I couldn't have called him anyway.

"Dearest, I don't want that child in the house putting ideas in Claire's head. God knows if she won't wander away again!"

Claire's father grunted.

Mrs. Bister went on, "Our daughter should not associate with such riffraff! He's odd! Coins from 1931, indeed! There's something very wrong about that child. Maxwell agrees. Darling, please call a cab and bring him over to the Boys' Home over on West One Hundred and First Street, there's a dear."

Coffee was served. The next minute we heard Robert Bister's voice on the house intercom. "That's right, Bruno," he said. "Whistle me down a yellow cab in five minutes. We're going to the west side. The driver can wait. Then it's home again. Evelyn and I have a party at midnight. We must dress."

I heard the familiar firm footsteps on the stairs. Claire's father was humming "Jingle Bells." He stopped to light his pipe. I could hear the click of his lighter. Above him one floor up Claire and I tore down the hall and back to Claire's room.

"Boys' home? What's that?" I asked desperately. "An orphanage? A loony bin? A reform school?"

"All three!" said Claire miserably.

"But Claire, if I'm put in the Boys' Home, I'll never see my dad again."

Tears glittering in her eyes, Claire knelt in front of the train. "This is the only way, Oscar," she said. "Get ready—he's coming up the stairs to get you."

"Wait!" I said. "My wallet! It's in the maid's room, in the pocket of my pants. All my tickets are

in it! They'll throw me off the train if I don't have a ticket!"

Claire leapt up and ran to her bureau. On top was a china piggy bank. She smashed it and piled fat masses of money into my hands.

"Good-bye, Oscar!" she said. Her words caught in her throat, but she knelt again and pushed the Twentieth Century's forward switch.

Her father rapped on the bedroom door. "Oscar, are you in there?" he asked politely, and knocked again.

"Come with me, Claire!" I suddenly yelled. I shoved the money in my pockets and reached out for her hand. "Jump, Claire," I shouted. "Jump!"

The door to her bedroom swung open. But Robert Bister was a second too late. Arms forward like a swan diver, I jumped clear and high into the New York City heavens. Claire's hand slipped out of mine at the last minute. Claire, her bedroom, and her father faded from me like stars in a sunrise.

CHAPTER 17

"Good morning, Mr. Moneybags!" said a familiar singsong voice.

The smell in my mouth and nose was sickening, yet I had smelled it before: Lysol disinfectant combined with canned fish sticks. Pure hospital. I opened my eyes and looked to see how far down in the bed my feet went. Was I six, or some other age? My feet poked up under the coverlet, at about four feet and five inches from my chin. I was eleven years old again, my real self. I tried to sigh with relief, but my chest was locked in heavy tape. I was hooked up to a dripping bag attached to a tube attached to a needle that was taped to my hand. This was alarming.

"Is that needle really stuck in your hand for good?" asked the voice at the head of my bed. It was Willa Sue.

I couldn't answer her. "Where am I?" I rasped. But if Willa Sue was here . . . and this was a hospital, then it could only be—sure enough, the sheets were all embroidered CAIRO METHODIST HOSPITAL. "Where's my dad?" I asked.

"He's on his way back from California," said Willa Sue. "Mama had quite a time reaching him. Did you know your dad was working on an orange ranch picking oranges? He quit his job because you're such a moneybags now. He'll be here tonight." Willa Sue looked no older than when I last saw her little Cutie Curls.

"When they found you on the sidewalk outside the station, Mama sent him a whole Western Union telegram all the way to Indian Grove Ranch in California telling him to get on home. It cost her three dollars and forty cents for one telegram!"

"When did this happen, Willa Sue?"

"Oh," said Willa Sue airily. "Mama has been up

with you for two days, while you were in that awful, disgusting steam tent. I had to stay overnight at the neighbors' house, and I didn't like it one bit."

"What happened then, Willa Sue?" I asked.

"Well," she answered primly, "you almost died, but you didn't."

I couldn't tell whether Willa Sue was happy or sad about that. "Mama's down in the cafeteria getting a cup of tea, so you just have me," she said, and kicked her legs, which did not yet reach the floor from the visitor's chair. On either side of Willa Sue were her favorite dolls. She patted them and adjusted them as if they were in our conversation.

"How did I almost die?" I asked Willa Sue.

"You've got four broken ribs. One! Two! Three! Four! Plus you have a punctured lung, just like a popped balloon," said Willa Sue. "It gave you new-monia, and you had a fever of one hundred and four degrees for all this time since they found you lying on the sidewalk outside the Chicago Station in a pair of Brooks Brothers Boys' Shop pajamas. Aunt Carmen said the pajamas must have cost a small fortune."

I was as weak as a bunny. That was true. "What's

the *Mr. Moneybags* all about?" I asked Willa Sue drowsily.

"Well," she said, "I'm not supposed to know, but I was hiding in that little coat closet and I heard everything! You were at death's door. They said you were in a croma—"

"Coma," I corrected her.

"The FBI detective was here," said Willa Sue. "The one with the glass eye."

"Pearly Gates!" I said.

"So that's why he's called Pearly," said Willa Sue.

"Never mind that, Willa Sue. What happened?"

"Well, Detective Pearly took one look at you and he said, 'What happened to the kid? Did he jump out of a ten-story window?' and right on the word *jump*, you opened your eyes and started talking a mile a minute. Even though you had a fever of one hundred and four degrees, you told him all about the bank robbery.

" 'We're gonna nab those goons!' That's the way Detective Pearly said it, and *Boom!* They did nab 'em, right on the Mexican border with only minutes to spare, and now, of course, Mr. Pettishanks is going to give you a big reward. Ten million dollars!"

"Thousand," I corrected.

"Ten something," said Willa Sue. "Monday morning, Mr. Pettishanks'll give you the check. It's a lot of money. You don't have to live with us anymore. I hope you buy me a present, Oscar."

"I'll get you a new doll, Willa Sue," I promised.

Willa Sue smiled her cutie-pie smile. "Oscar," she asked, "what's so special about the word *jump?*"

I did not answer Willa Sue. I had slid back toward the warm hands of sleep. But on cue my memory of the last two days kicked in and began trickling back to me. I could remember the fever, the pneumonia, and the steam tent.

I could see Detective Gates writing furiously in his notepad. "Stackpole!" I wailed to him through my illness. "Stackpole and McGee! Stackpole was bent over like a monkey; mustache and bad complexion. McGee was a little runt with red hair. They were going to head to El Paso and then to Mexico. I tried to help Mr. Applegate!" Here my recollection was gauzy. Detective Gates wanted to know who Mr. Applegate was.

"He was the night watchman," I'd insisted.

"There weren't no night watchmen," said Detective Pearly Gates.

This puzzled me, but I didn't want to ask Willa Sue or Aunt Carmen anything about it. Willa Sue left my hospital room holding Aunt Carmen's hand. They promised to be back with my dad as soon as he came in on the train.

The nurse brought lunch. Crumbed fish loaf. I left the meal untouched under its metal lid, congealing on a tray beside my bed, until midafternoon when I woke.

On my tray I saw there was today's paper, neatly folded. I opened the paper to the front page. It was January 3, 1932. I had been gone only ten days. Dad was still at Indian Grove. The Tip-Top Ranch was years in the future, and there was no war being fought. Everything was normal, and best of all, my dad was on his way. The front headline read:

DOUBLE CRIME SPREE
GOONS NABBED
ROBBERY!
KIDNAPPING SOLVED!

Double? I said to myself. *Double?* I read on with curiosity.

Jan. 2, 1932—Detective Gates of the Federal Bureau of Investigation announced last night at approximately 5:00 p.m. that two thugs, Mickey Stackpole and Buck McGee, were apprehended by police in El Paso, Texas, just as they were about to cross the border into Mexico. They had with them almost every dollar of the $50,000 stolen from the First National Bank in Cairo on Christmas Eve. Stackpole and McGee are two-time losers, according to Detective Gates. He expects they will get life imprisonment in a maximum-security jail. The two are charged with grand larceny and kidnapping.

As this paper reported yesterday, the eleven-year-old boy whom the thugs kidnapped was discovered outside Chicago's Union Station and was in critical condition. His condition has been upgraded to good. At this edition of the paper, the boy, Oscar Ogilvie of Cairo, was able to identify and name the perpetrators in question. The reward offered by the bank's owner will be paid in full. "I am a gratified man," Mr. Pettishanks of the First National Bank was quoted as saying.

I asked the empty air, "But what about Mr. Applegate? Did he disappear from the face of the earth? He was certainly not in the bank that night, not anymore. He wasn't murdered, either. Where was he?"

The nurse peeked her head around the doorway.

"You have a visitor!" she chirped. "Are you strong enough to eat a little chocolate?"

Chocolate? Who would send me chocolate? I waited for the visitor to appear. He shambled into the room, ruddy-cheeked, shirt rumpled, and looking embarrassed. He carried a Whitman's sampler box, which he had clearly broken into somewhere along the line. It was Cyril. It being just New Year's 1932, he was, of course, just his fifth-grade self. He had not yet set foot in Missouri Military Prep. Cyril was exactly ten years short of being a vengeful meany in a lieutenant's uniform.

"My father made me come," said Cyril, "seeing you won the reward and all." He looked at my intravenous tubing, and the color drained out of his cheeks. He handed me the dented box of chocolates. "He sent you these as a get-well thing. Sorry, I opened the box and had a couple in the elevator."

"I'm sorry I made you look bad, Cyril," I said. "That day with Kipling's 'If.' I didn't mean to make it go rough for you."

"That's okay," said Cyril, looking at the floor and putting his hands in his pockets. "Is that a needle going into your hand?"

"Yup," I answered.

"Wow!" he said, and sat on the floor instead of the chair.

In my bed, knowing what I knew would happen someday, I wondered if Cyril could possibly ever grow up into a nice man if his father didn't send him off to military school in the fifth grade. "Cyril," I said, "I have something you might want to see."

"Yeah?" he asked.

"See my blue coat hanging on the hook behind the door? Go in the pocket. Take a look."

Cyril got up. "It's the fricking poem," he said. "But it's . . . it's all written funny."

"It's the code to memorizing," I told him. "You set up anchor words. You memorize them. Then the rest of it comes easy as 'Pop Goes the Weasel.'"

Cyril tried it. "This works!" Cyril said. "My God, Ogilvie! This works!"

We finished the whole box of chocolates and the whole poem. Cyril smiled and shook my un-needled hand.

"Good job, Ogilvie," he said. "It's enough to keep me out of Missouri Military Prep, anyway!"

My dad rolled home on a night train. He took a cab to the hospital in spite of Aunt Carmen's telling him to wait for the bus. He had a California suntan, fruit pickers' blistered hands, and a grin like a Christmas tree on his face.

"Dad!" I shouted. "I wish I could touch you!" I couldn't because of my ribs and my needle. Was he real?

"Oscar!" said Dad. "You're okay! I thought you were dead!"

"Dad," I marveled at him. He was the dad I knew again, not old and tired-looking. I sputtered out, "Your hair! It's back!"

Dad ran his fingers through his thick hair, puzzled. "Oscar?" he picked up my pain medication and examined it. "What's in those pills?"

Dad stayed with me, sleeping in a hospital chair

next to my bed until I was released. We went to the bank Monday morning and retrieved the check from Mr. Pettishanks himself.

"Gonna buy the old house back, Ogilvie?" Mr. Pettishanks wanted to know.

"Don't think so," said my dad. "Think Oscar and I'll buy an orange ranch in the valley of L.A. county, California."

"Sir," I piped up, "may I ask you something?"

Mr. Pettishanks smiled his dry smile. "Fire away, boy."

"Was there . . . wasn't there a night watchman called Applegate in the bank the night of the robbery?"

Mr. Pettishanks frowned. "Applegate? Never heard of him. The watchman's name was George Perkins, and he was hiding in the basement washroom the whole time. I fired him! Good luck to you, fella," said Mr. Pettishanks, and he handed my dad a big Macanudo.

We put the check for ten thousand dollars in Dad's bank account. Then first thing, we went to the car dealer and bought Aunt Carmen a new Buick so she could drive to her clients' houses. Then we called the phone company and ordered a telephone for her front hallway.

"You are wasting money again, Oscar!" Aunt Carmen scolded him, but she scolded him with some June in those January blue eyes.

"A car is peanuts compared to an orange ranch in El Segundo, California," said Dad. "As for the phone, me and Oscar'll call you every Sunday night and chat from California!"

We moved in with Aunt Carmen and Willa Sue until a bungalow was built for us on the Red Star Ranch in El Segundo, California.

On the afternoon that the telephone was installed at Aunt Carmen's, I waited until I was alone. I looked in the brand-new telephone book that came with the phone and found the number for the Cairo YMCA, and made a phone call.

"YMCA," answered a bored voice.

"Could you tell me if you have a Harold Applegate staying at the Y?" I asked.

"Ah . . . let's see," said the voice. It trailed off. "Nah . . . Armon, Angleweiss, but no Applegates."

"Could you possibly tell me when he moved out?" I asked.

"Ah c'mon, kid. I gotta lot of men come and go. I don't keep track of 'em. That stuff's in the old records in the main office."

"Maybe he left a forwarding address," I said. "I'm his nephew and I've been looking for him a long while. Is there any way you could check?"

The telephone seemed to go dead. Had the man hung up on me? Five minutes passed, and then the voice came back through the receiver. "Yup. He paid his room through November twenty-first last year. No forwarding address. But he ain't had no mail. That's all I got, kid. Bye."

Dad and I ordered all the Lionel trains we had owned before. We set up a temporary layout in Aunt Carmen's basement.

"We'll have 'em all shipped out to El Segundo soon, Oscar," Dad promised. "We're going to have the best darn layout you've ever seen out there. I told the builder we wanted a big basement in that bungalow of ours!"

"It'll be better than the Crawford layout!" I said. "Bigger and better." But since it was only 1932, Dad had no memory of the Crawford layout, or of Dutch,

Mr. H., or anything else that was to happen in the next ten years. He just looked at me funny, just as he would when I slipped and mentioned something that had not yet happened and maybe never would.

We stayed on in Cairo until I could keep my promise to Aunt Carmen to memorize and perform a recitation on the Fourth of July. Then everyone in town would know what a terrific declamation tutor she was.

I didn't like the Gettysburg Address, or anything in *Famous Speeches of Famous Men*. It was all much too long and boring. I was determined to find a poem and recite it in Mr. Applegate's honor, wherever he might be.

One day in the Cairo Library, on the highest shelf in the poetry stacks, I spotted the shabby spine of *The Fireside Book of Poetry*. I wheeled over a stepladder and took the book down. Leafing through, to my surprise I found that someone had written in the book. There were words in red pen over the top of Kipling's poem. I knew that page. Last time I saw it, the book had been left in Aunt Carmen's kitchen by Mr. Applegate. There had certainly been

nothing scrawled on the "If" page when Mr. Applegate showed it to me in the glider on Aunt Carmen's
front porch.

Suddenly my breath quickened. I recognized the
handwriting, the crisp block letters written perfectly
as if with a ruler. The message said:

MR. APPLEGATE! DON'T EVER TAKE A JOB
IN A BANK. DON'T EVER WORK FOR A MAN
NAMED PETTISHANKS OR YOU WILL DIE BY
GUNSHOT DURING A ROBBERY!

My pulse hammered so that I could feel it in my
ears. I flipped to the back of the book cover. I opened
the card sleeve and ran my finger down the checkout
dates. As before, all the dates were stamped in order.
September 1931, October 1931, November 1931. Then,
completely out of order, came the last checkout date,
January 3, 1926. How could that be?

"Claire!" I shouted into the dusty stillness of
the library. "*Claire.* You were here! You saved Mr.
Applegate!"

Before the librarian could stride back into the
stacks and find out what was wrong with me, I

scrawled at the bottom of the same page, *Gone to Red Star Ranch, El Segundo, California. Come on out!*

Someday I knew Claire would start up the Twentieth Century and fill its smokestack with pellets. She'd come to Cairo and know just where to find *The Fireside Book of Poetry*.

I crept past the librarian at her desk on my way out, nodding politely, which she did back to me. I was such a good boy, using the library to prepare for that Fourth of July recitation. I would never yell in the stacks or write in a library book.

Dad was waiting for me under one of the big library elms. He hadn't let me too far out of his sight since the hospital. He got to his feet and broke into a whistle. He was still a bushy-haired man, my dad, with an easy walk and a strong hand on my shoulder. I grinned back up at him and we went downtown to Mr. Kinoshura's drugstore to have a soda.

On the streets of Cairo, jobs were as rare as hen's teeth. There was a shabbiness to people's clothes and fear in their eyes because of the crash. But according to my dad, a man named Frank Roosevelt was setting up to run for president and make things better

for the people in the country. I wanted so much to tell my dad that Mr. Roosevelt would succeed. He'd stand up on his two feet in spite of his polio and get the country back on the tracks again.

In the meantime, Dad and I were soon to head for California, land of surprises. "I've got us two sleeper seats on the Golden State for July fifth night," Dad said and fished in his pocket to show them to me. "It leaves from Dearborn Station in Chicago at 7:09. You've never been on such a grand train in your life, Oscar," he said. "Never in your life."

I didn't argue. Mr. Kinoshura made us two chocolate sodas. Nobody hated the Japanese yet, or even the Germans. No one was in a soldier's or sailor's uniform, and nowhere could we hear the voice of the wolf.